COMPLETELY CASSIDY

DRAMA QUEEN

For Loughton Operatic Society,

who make THESPING so much fun.

First published in 2016 by Usborne Publishing Ltd.,
Usborne House, 83-85 Saffron Hill, London EC1N 8RT, England.
www.usborne.com

Copyright © Tamsyn Murray, 2016

The right of Tamsyn Murray to be identified as the author
of this work has been asserted by her in accordance with the
Copyright, Designs and Patents Act, 1988.

Cover and inside illustrations by Antonia Miller.
Title lettering by Stephen Raw.

The name Usborne and the devices ♈ 🎈 are Trade Marks of
Usborne Publishing Ltd.

All rights reserved. No part of this publication may be reproduced, stored in a
retrieval system or transmitted in any form or by any means, electronic, mechanical,
photocopying, recording or otherwise without the prior permission of the publisher.

This is a work of fiction. The characters, incidents, and dialogues are products of the
author's imagination and are not to be construed as real. Any resemblance to actual
events or persons, living or dead, is entirely coincidental.

A CIP catalogue record for this book is available from the British Library.

JFMAM JASOND/16

ISBN 9781474906999 03965/04

Printed in the UK.

COMPLETELY CASSIDY

DRAMA QUEEN

USBORNE

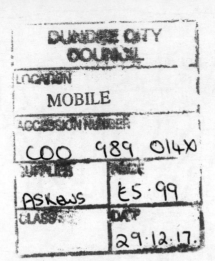

DUNDEE CITY
COUNCIL

LOCATION

MOBILE

ACCESSION NUMBER

COO 989 014X

SUPPLIER

ASKews

PRICE

£5.99

CLASS

DATE

29.12.17.

Eton Dorney Dance and Drama Academy
Where the Stars of Tomorrow Start Shining!

APPLICATION FORM

Thank you for choosing EDDDA.

We believe that every child deserves the chance to be a star and there's no better place to shine than with us. With more than fifty years' experience in all areas of stagecraft, our staff will nurture your child's inner sparkle and polish it until they are nothing short of brilliant – all in four short weeks.

If your child prefers to stay out of the limelight, we teach stage management, make-up magic and costume design too – there's something for everyone!

I look forward to welcoming your budding Brads and Angelinas very soon.

Best wishes,
Elenora Skelly
Principal

Cassidy, how much is this going to cost? Mum xx

<u>NAME</u>: Cassidy Bond   <u>AGE</u>: Nearly 12

<u>EXPERIENCE</u>:

* Sheep #2 in school nativity play
  aged 5 (non-baa-ing role)
* 80% accuracy on several
  Singstar songs

<u>SPECIAL TALENTS</u>:

Still searching for my THING but can;
* Lick my own elbow
* Make a balloon poodle (although sometimes more
  of a sausage-poo)
* Change a wet nappy in less than thirty seconds

NB: Can't dance but can hula-hoop

Specialist subject = Harry Potter

CHAPTER ONE

Ugh, it is too hot.

I know it is July and supposed to be sunny but it said on the news that the temperature in England is hotter than Greece, which I can totally believe. Rolo spends all his time lying flat on the floor, panting like he has just conquered Everest, the twins seem to be in training for **THE GREAT BRITISH GRUMP OFF** and apparently the roads might melt if it goes on much longer, which is not going to help with anything. How will the ice cream van get down our street with much-needed supplies if the tarmac is streaming like molten lava?

"It's because of climate change," Shenice told us as we dragged our sweaty, overheated selves home from school one blistering Tuesday afternoon near the end of term.

"Climate change?" Molly asked, fanning her face with a wilting copy of the Year Seven newsletter. "Is that like the French exchange programme but with weather instead of students?"

Shenice shook her head. "No, it means the world is getting hotter and we have no one to blame but ourselves. Thanks to Man's selfish actions, the planet is heating up and basically we're all doomed unless we take positive action to stop it now."

Eek. I glanced sideways at Molly — this wasn't what

we usually talked about on the way home from school.
Normally, we argue about who is the hottest member of
THE DROIDS or whether Mr Peterson's lessons could get
any duller, but ever since Shenice's mum went on
a big demonstration march in London
last month, she's been all about
the environmental
friendliness and a tiny bit is
rubbing off on Shenice.
I can't see how men could be
causing the entire earth to overheat,
though, no matter how selfish they are – although now
I come to think of it, some of Liam's farts are pretty
toxic. I know older brothers are supposed to be gross
but he is off the charts disgusting so I can totally see
how he might contribute to the end of life as we know
it. My little brother, Joshua, is less to blame – even the
hardest eco-warrior wouldn't blame an eight-month-old
baby for the pollution his bottom emits. And then
it dawned on me that Shenice meant MAN as a species,

not men as individuals, and everything made a lot
more sense.

"What kind of action?" Molly asked.

"Walking instead of driving, buying locally sourced
food, washing clothes at a lower temperature," Shenice
replied, ticking the items off on her fingers. "But our
biggest challenge is climate-change deniers. Did you know
that there are actually idiots who refuse to believe
there's a problem?"

I thought about that. No one who'd smelled one of
Liam's eye-watering efforts could deny that he had
a problem.

"Huh," Molly said. "We should invite them to spend
a day at St Jude's. Is it just me or is it hotter there than
anywhere else?"

I have to admit I felt a tiny bit guilty then. St Jude's DOES feel hotter than the sun at the moment but that's mostly because all three of us are wearing trousers in a heatwave. Ever since I started a petition to allow girls to wear trousers to school and the school governors changed the rules to say we can, I have felt like I cannot ever be TROUSERLESS. And Molly and Shenice are being brilliant BFFs and supporting me, in spite of some serious perspiration problems. Leading a revolution is much sweatier than I expected.

"At least it's nearly the end of term," I said. "Just think, no more Mr Peterson for six whole weeks."

It's not that I don't like maths but Mr Peterson is to fun what my dad is to coolness: a vacuum. Although at least Mr Peterson doesn't dress up as Elvis Presley in his spare time like Dad. Honestly, it's like he is on a mission to win Most Embarrassing Parent EVER. He's even talking about taking his tufty black wig and sparkly white onesie on holiday with us to Happy Sands this year. I am going to live with Aunt Jane and Uncle Ian if he does.

"No more Mrs Pitt-Rivers," Shenice said, shivering in spite of the heat.

Mrs Pitt-Rivers is our super-strict Deputy Headteacher – seriously, she makes Miss Trunchbull look relaxed. I don't mind her so much since she was almost nice to me a few months ago but Shenice is terrified of her.

"No more Nathan Crossfield," Molly pointed out, with a sideways look at me. "Unless there's something you're not telling us?"

My cheeks were already warm but they suddenly became fiery hot. Nathan Crossfield is the most popular boy in Year Seven – he's the football team's star striker, a favourite with the teachers and the closest thing St Jude's Secondary has to a celebrity. He's also my favourite person to share a sundae with and I might have an eensy-weensy crush on him. Oh, and I once threw up on his feet, but we NEVER talk about that.

"I don't know what you mean," I said, trying to make like Queen Elsa and think frosty thoughts. "Nathan who?"

"Oh, purlease," Molly said, rolling her eyes. "Are you seeing him over the summer holidays or not?"

"How can she?" Shenice asked. "The summer course at Eton Dorney Dance and Drama Academy starts as soon as school finishes and she's going to Happy Sands for a week. She won't have time."

I do have a teensy little CONFESSION to make here:
I'm not sure I'll even be going to EDDDA. I know we all
agreed to sign up for it but that was before Mum saw
the cost. She sighed so hard that our neighbours must
have thought we'd been struck by some kind of extremely
localized mini-hurricane. And then I'd heard her arguing
with Dad about it after I'd gone to bed. Mum said we
didn't have the money, not on top of our trip to Cornwall,
and Dad said it was about time I got in touch with my
inner Elvis, which made me suddenly feel a LOT less keen.
But Molly and Shenice are SUPER-EXCITED about it and
it's giving me serious FOMO – Fear Of Missing Out.
I am really hoping acting will be my BIG TALENT. I read
somewhere that the best actors are called THESPIANS
and it seems to me that it will be a lot harder to win
an Oscar if I never get the chance to THESP. But short
of winning the lottery, I can't see how I'm going to get
to EDDDA.

Obviously, I hadn't quite worked up the courage to

give my BFFs the bad news – I'd been pinning my hopes on a last-minute miracle. What makes it worse is that Nathan won't be around either – he told me last week that his dad is working in Australia for the whole of the summer break and Nathan has to go too. Six weeks without a visit to the Shake Shack. Forty-two days without a SUGAR RUSH MOUNTAIN. 1,008 long hours without the cutest smile outside of THE DROIDS. I hadn't told Molly and Shenice that either because I was secretly hoping I'd wake up and find the whole conversation had been a bad dream. But the time had come to face facts: my summer was about to become a FRIEND-FREE ZONE.

"Oh," Molly said, when I told them about Nathan now. "That sucks."

Shenice nodded in sympathy. "It does. But EDDDA is going to be so much fun!"

"Yeah," I said, making a wish and hoping my fairy godmother was paying attention. "Well, I've got some not-so-brilliant news about that too..."

By the time we reached the end of my road, I'd managed to drag them down to my level and none of us could find a silver lining. I said a gloomy goodbye before trudging to my front door. I wouldn't be surprised if they have such a good time THESPING that they forget who I am by the time September rolls around. If only I had something to look forward to instead of a week up close and personal with my family.

If only fairy godmothers were real.

Mum looked hot and harassed when I walked into the living room.

"Cassidy, Rolo ate another pair of your knickers

 this morning," she said, blowing her fringe off her sticky-looking forehead as she wrestled with a wriggling Ethel. "You're going to have to start putting them into your washing basket instead of leaving them on the floor."

Rolo looked up at the mention of his name and wagged his tail in case it was followed by a "Good boy!" I don't know what's worse – his obsession with my underwear or having to discuss it with my mother. She doesn't seem to get that Rolo only eats clean, freshly washed pants. He likes his food peppered with Persil so it doesn't matter how untidy my room is. Even so, the situation is reaching RED ALERT: I am running out of underwear. Any minute now it is going to trigger another of Mum's "We-Are-Not-Made-of-Money" lectures. I KNOW we don't have much money – you only have to look in the cupboards and see the woefully low levels of chocolate and other essentials – but I can't help it if Rolo noses out my knickers with all the instincts of a police sniffer dog, can I? He finds them wherever I put them – NOWHERE is safe.

Something thudded against my foot. I looked down to see Joshua half-wedged under the table, his chunky little legs waggling like flippers. Ever since the twins started crawling, Mum's had her work cut out keeping them out of mischief. It's like they're eight-month-old criminal masterminds – one of them creates a distraction and the other commits the heist. Joshua's crime of choice is stealing the biscuits from Rolo's bowl. Actually, it is no wonder Rolo is eating my KNICKERS – he's probably starving most of the time.

"I spoke to Miss Skelly, the principal of the drama academy today, about course fees," Mum said as I rescued Joshua and swung him into my arms. He had a Cheerio stuck to his forehead, making him look like an extra from MONSTERS, INC.

"Okay," I said, fending off his determined effort to thrust his fingers up my nostrils. This was it – make or break time for my summer, and quite possibly my entire future. "And?"

Mum took a deep breath. My heart sank. It couldn't be good news, not when her face looked like a gloomy black cloud. "Apparently, they have a bursary for students who can't afford the full fee. We had a chat about our family circumstances and it seems we qualify. They want a reference from St Jude's so I gave them Mr Bearman's name."

"Oh," I said, and my last hope vanished like a snowflake on a barbecue. Of all the teachers at St Jude's, Mr Bearman is my favourite, but I can't help thinking I've been a bit of a disappointment to him so far. First there was the time when the school thought I was a genius and I turned out not to be, and second there was the whole mess with the school magazine, where EVERYONE thought I was a gossip queen when I totally wasn't. So although Mr Bearman is really nice (for a teacher), I don't think he's likely to recommend me for a drama school bursary. Not when he thinks I am a DISASTER ON LEGS.

Mum jiggled Ethel around on one hip. "I'm sorry we can't pay for all of it like Molly and Shenice's parents. It's just that money's a bit—"

"Tight at the moment," I finished for her, trying hard not to picture a summer where the highlight of the holidays was a treasure hunt around Happy Sands with their mascot, Captain Pigeon. "Yeah, I know."

"Well, don't lose hope," Mum said, sniffing at Ethel's bottom. "Sorry, Rolo, I thought that smell was you. Back in a minute."

She disappeared upstairs, carrying my stinky little sister with her. I sat down with Joshua and looked into his big, round eyes. "Peekaboo," I said glumly.

"Bah!" he said, before letting rip with the loudest burp I have ever heard in my life. I swear the windows rattled a bit. Looking ridiculously pleased with himself, he gurgled happily and threw up, covering my shirt with half-digested dog biscuits.

"MUM!" I bellowed, turning Joshua around in case he did it again. "YOUR SON IS THE MOST DISGUSTING CREATURE KNOWN TO HUMANITY!"

"Which one?" she shouted back.

I hesitated because even though Liam has never been sick on me, there are a hundred tiny ways he is worse than Joshua and Joshua is only a baby so can't be held totally responsible for his actions. "Both!" I yelled.

And then Rolo obviously decided he was going to get in on the DISGUSTINGNESS action because he started trying to lick the baby sick/biscuit combo off my shirt.

What's that old show-business saying – never work with children or animals? SIGN ME UP NOW.

To: <u>BondGirl007</u>

From: <u>WarrenWhite@HypnoHour</u>

Dear Cassidy,

Thank you for your email asking for some "Jedi mind tricks" to use on your teacher, Mr Bearman. While I can see that it would be a "DISASTER BEYOND BELIEF" if you were unable to attend drama school this summer, I'm afraid I can't give you advice on persuading people to do anything they do not want to do. I think you would be much better off showing this teacher how brilliant you are at acting and take things from there.

I do sympathize about the situation with your brother but sadly there isn't a hypnotist in the world who could help with his flatulence. Your concerns about being confined to a caravan with him certainly seem valid, however, so perhaps a trip to the doctor might be in order before your holiday or, failing that, a very large peg for your nose.

Thank you for your interest in hypnosis. Keep watching the show!

Kind regards,

Warren White

Hypnotist to the Stars

CHAPTER TWO

"Have you got a minute, please, Cassie?"

Mr Bearman caught me at the end of English.
I trudged to the front of the class and told Molly and
Shenice to save me a seat in the canteen. This was it —
the moment where Mr Bearman exiled me to a summer
of deathly dullness. "Yes, sir?"

"I've been contacted by the principal of a local drama
school, asking whether I think you'd be a worthwhile

candidate for an acting bursary this summer." He studied me thoughtfully. "I didn't know you had ambitions to tread the boards."

"TREAD THE BOREDS"? That's what I'd be doing if I DIDN'T get the bursary. This was it – my big chance to convince him I had star quality.

"Oh yes, sir," I said airily. "To be or not to be, that is the question."

Mr Bearman smiled. "It's certainly one of them," he agreed, settling back into his chair. "So tell me, what would your dream role be?"

My mind was a total blank. Honestly, it was like someone had pulled the plug in my head and all my thoughts had gone swirling down the hole it had left.

I needed to come up with something FAST. Think, Cassidy, THINK. "Erm...Hermione Granger?"

"Good choice," Mr Bearman said, nodding. "And what would you bring to the role that no one else can?"

What? WHAT? I pictured Hermione – clever, resourceful, magical Hermione. And then I thought about me – average, accident-prone, occasionally baby-sick-covered Muggle me. Apart from our hair colour, we didn't have anything in common. In fact, we couldn't have been more different if one of us had been born a hippogriff.

I started to sweat. "Uh...well..." And then, as I wished for the eleventy-billionth time that I wasn't wearing trousers, inspiration struck. "I'd use my experience of starting the Battle for Equal Trousers to help me understand Hermione's campaign for house elf freedom, sir."

Mr Bearman studied me for a long moment. "That's a very good answer. Okay, Cassie, leave it with me. I'll get back to Miss Skelly this afternoon."

"Thanks, sir," I said, hoping I'd done enough to convince him. Because if I hadn't, I'd be TREADING THE BOREDS big time this summer.

OMG. OMG. OMG.

BEST. NEWS. EVER – Mr Bearman came through! Mum got a call from Miss Skelly and they've accepted me for the EDDDA bursary – I'm going to drama school! Molly and Shenice are over the moon too – our summer is going to totally ROCK. I'm already dreaming of the dress I'll wear to accept my Best Actress award and planning what I'll say in my speech – obviously, I'll thank Mr Bearman for giving me my first break, and my BFFs for being amazing, and Rolo for being the best dog ever (even if he does eat my

knickers and is sometimes gross beyond belief)
and...and...my parents, of course, for setting my feet
on the sparkly road to superstardom, although if Dad
thinks he is wearing his Elvis costume to the ceremony,
he is in for a shock.

I am pretty excited about my new acting career.
I don't even mind so much that I am not going to see
Nathan for the 3,628,800 seconds while he is in Australia,
because I will be doing something pretty cool myself.

He seemed really pleased for me when I told him.

"Wow, Cassie, that's great news," he said, as we
were being dragged round the park by an enthusiastic Rolo
after school on the last day of term. "Molly showed me
the flyer ages ago – Mum even signed me up for the
stage-management course – but Dad's work trip means I
can't go. Australia will be amazing but it would have been
cool to spend the summer hanging out with you guys."

It would have been off-the-charts AMAZING to have had Nathan at the drama academy too — basically all my dreams come true. But Australia seemed like an awesome place to visit — it definitely outshone my holiday destination. I doubted he'd be sharing a duvet with the WORLD'S MADDEST DOG, either.

"I'm sure you'll have a fantastic time," I said, trying to ignore a little niggle of sadness. "You won't miss us at all."

He looked at me weirdly for a minute then, like he was trying to work something out. "I'll have my phone with me. Maybe I could send you an email every now and then, to let you know what I've been up to."

I nodded. "Yeah, and I could tell you how drama

school is going. Fill you in on all the breaking Windsor news."

He smiled at me in a way that made my tummy go all squiggly. "I'd like that."

The park seemed to melt away then, leaving just me and Nathan smiling at each other. Dimly, I felt Rolo's extendable lead vibrate in my fingers but I was too busy staring into Nathan's bright blue eyes and wondering if it would be cheesy to hold his hand for the rest of the walk. And then—

BAM!

My arm was practically wrenched from its socket as the lead jerked out of my hand and Rolo took off across the grass. "Rolo, no!" I yelled.

In the distance, I could just about make out another

dog, so far away that it looked like a toy. I couldn't tell what breed it was but Rolo had a history of picking the biggest, growliest dogs to go lolloping up to. Groaning, I started to run. "Come back here, you stupid dog! Rolo! Rolo, HEEL!"

He didn't listen. I don't know how we managed it but we seem to have chosen an untrainable dog. Nathan was keeping up with me as I panted after Rolo. I knew without looking that he wouldn't even be out of breath — he played football for the school team, this was nothing. I also knew that I looked a lot like a sweaty red tomato. But there was nothing I could do about that now — if we didn't catch Rolo, he'd be out of the gates and onto the streets and then I'd have a real problem. Even though he is microchipped, Rolo has less road awareness than the twins.

"ROLO, SIT DOWN!" I bellowed, but it was no use. Rolo was hearing the call of the wild, not the desperate screeching of his owner. And then something caught his nose and he slowed down to sniff.

"Pincer movement!" Nathan whispered. "You go right and I'll go left."

He peeled off to my left, circling around to the side of Rolo. I crept in the other direction, trying to get enough oxygen into my lungs without panting so loud I scared my dog. Nathan reached into his pocket. "What's this I've got, Rolo? Is it cheese?"

Rolo's ears shot up. He twisted around to look at Nathan, his nose still stuck to whatever it was he could smell on the grass. I knew Nathan couldn't really have cheese in his pocket – Rolo would have been all over him the moment we'd met him if he had – but it was a great distraction while I sneaked around the back.

"What's this, boy?" Nathan said, rustling a piece of paper. "Have I got some lovely cheddar for you?"

Now Rolo lifted his head, his tail wagging like crazy. In a few seconds' time, he was going to take the bait and rush over to Nathan. Taking a deep breath, I launched myself towards him, grabbing the dangling lead and bundling him to the floor. "Got you!"

Rolo let out a yelp of surprise. "Bad dog!" I said in a voice that made his ears droop and his tail sink to the floor. "Naughty Rolo."

"Aw, don't be too hard on him," Nathan said, flopping to the grass beside Rolo. "He'll grow out of the naughtiness eventually."

"When?" I asked, blowing my sticky fringe off my forehead. "By the time he's ten, do you think?"

Nathan laughed. "No idea." He glanced sideways at me and my stomach did that weird flip-flop thing again. "But I think we made a pretty good team just now. I'm going to miss you when I'm away."

"I'm going to miss you too," I said.

He reached for my hand to pull me up.

And his fingers held mine all the way home.

Geography Holiday Project:

Choose a country other than the UK and find out some
interesting facts about it.

Total COINCIDENCE
that Nathan happens
to be going here...

Cassie's Awesome Australia Facts

* Australia is the smallest continent in the world.

* Two thirds of the country is desert, and is known as
  the Outback.

* Most people think Sydney is the capital city but it is
  actually Canberra.

* There are around a hundred types of venomous snakes
  in Australia – EEK!

* There are about forty kinds of funnel-web spiders –
  DOUBLE EEK! (Note to self: only six are dangerous)

* Australia is home to loads of animals that don't live anywhere else – koalas, kangaroos, kookaburras (why do they all begin with K?).

* Kids who live in the remotest parts of Australia don't go to school – they have internet classrooms instead – SO LUCKY!

* Australia is on the opposite side of the world, so when it's summer for us, it's winter for them – I wonder if Nathan knows this?

* It snows in Australia – they even have their own Alps!

To: <u>BondGirl007</u>

From: <u>Happy Sands Enquiries</u>

Hi Cassie,

Thanks for getting in touch again – we're really looking forward to welcoming you to Happy Sands Newquay this summer!

I'm delighted to be able to tell you that we're very green here. Our caravans are all eco-friendly and powered by our fabulous solar-powered Sunbeam Paddock, and we encourage our guests to use the recycling bins located across the park. On Monday mornings, Crusty and the Crab Crew lead a beach-combing expedition to help keep the sands of our nearest beach clean, and they're always looking for happy helpers. There's even a Surf Skool if you want to get wet!

In answer to your other question, I don't think we

can enforce a No Elvis rule in the clubhouse as all our guests are welcome to dress however they choose. So I'm afraid I cannot promise to refuse your dad entry if he wears the "ridiculous onesie and wig" outfit you describe.

Not long now – just two weeks to go!

High Fives and Hang Tens,

Tracy Cooper
Head of Children's Entertainment, Happy Sands Holiday Villages PLC

Memo to self:
Hide Dad's Elvis wigs

CHAPTER THREE

What's that thing old people say — be careful what you wish for? I could kind of see what they meant because I woke up on the morning of the first day at EDDDA, suddenly terrified I had made a MASSIVE mistake. I blame Liam for being such a pig when I brushed past him on my way to bed the night before.

"I hear you're so stupid you have to go to school in the summer holidays," he taunted me.

I looked down my nose at him in a haughty fashion, which was actually quite hard as he is much taller than me so I had to tip my head back to get the desired effect. "It's drama academy, actually. Shame Mum and Dad can't get a bursary to send you to personality school."

He clicked his fingers in what I suppose he thought was a cool way. "They don't need to, I'm already Mr Charisma. Just ask your mate Molly."

There wasn't much I could say to that – Molly is totally blinkered by LOVE GOGGLES where Liam is concerned and she refuses to hear a bad word against him. It doesn't matter how often I remind her what a SUPER-DORK he is, she just doesn't get it. The really annoying thing is that his band, WOLF BRETHREN, are pretty good, especially since Anjel joined as their new guitarist and toned down some of their more dubious lyrics. Not that I'd admit any of that to Liam, of course.

"Molly is completely insane," I told him. "She's not a reliable witness to anything."

"What can I say? You've either got star quality or you haven't." He leaned closer. "And just so we're clear, you haven't."

"We'll see about that," I said, glaring at him. "Hey, wouldn't it be hilarious if it turned out I'm better at performing than you?"

He snorted. "You've certainly got a talent for embarrassing yourself. Remember when Mum took you to Twinkletoes dance classes and you stamped on that girl's foot and broke her metatarsal?"

That was a low blow – who didn't have trouble telling their left from their right when they were five?

"They probably won't even let you through the door,

especially if word has got around about
what an EGGHEAD you are."

I frowned. Did he mean the time
I was accidentally declared a genius?
Or the time I'd rinsed my hair with
raw eggs and ended up on JUICE
ON JUDE'S, the school gossip website? Honestly, he makes
it sound like I am a CRINGE-MAGNET when really these
things just happen. "No one even remembers that."

Liam laughed. "Everyone remembers that. Let's face
it, Cass, you're comedy gold."

He's not wrong — Molly and Shenice think I am
HILARIOUS. And then I realized there's a difference
between people laughing at a joke you've made and people
laughing at YOU.

"Imagine having one of your SPECIAL LITTLE

MOMENTS onstage, though," Liam went on, sounding as though he was starting to enjoy himself. "Imagine how it will feel with all those new people watching you mess everything up. Because you will. You always do eventually."

As much as I hate to say this, there's an eensy-weensy chance he's got a point – disaster does have a habit of finding me. Which is why I'm not looking forward to uncovering my inner superstar at EDDDA this morning. I don't think she wants to be uncovered – in fact, I think she's got stage fright.

Is it too late to change my mind?

Shenice was all for walking on our first day but, as the school where EDDDA is being held is about three miles away from where we live and it was raining, there was no way I was going along with that. Liam's taunts were still buzzing in my ears, like little CONFIDENCE-CHOMPING MOSQUITOES, and the last thing I needed was to turn up looking like I'd lost a fight with a rain cloud. So we all piled into Molly's mum's car instead, which is one of those hybrid things – not the kind that turns → into a robot, thankfully, but the kind that runs partly on petrol and partly on electricity so at least we weren't totally dealing the planet a death blow.

Molly's excitement had reached fever pitch already and we hadn't even got halfway there yet. "On a scale of one to ten, how AWESOME is this?" she squeaked.

"Ten!" Shenice squealed back. "No – wait – ELEVEN!"

They both looked at me and I dredged up enough
enthusiasm to say, "Yay!"

Shenice was so far into the EXCITEMENT ZONE that
she completely missed my lack of squee. She turned to
Molly. "What do you think it's going to be like?"

She shrugged. "It's being held in a performing arts
school so there'll be a stage and rehearsal rooms and
probably even dance studios. The last drama course I did
had a show at the end and all the parents came to watch."

Shen's eyes gleamed. "It sounds brilliant. Imagine
if everyone just bursts into song whenever they feel
like it."

My feet were getting so cold they could have single-
handedly stopped global warming. Molly is an amazing
singer – she has lessons and everyone agrees she's got
what it takes – but I'm pretty sure singing isn't my

thing. Even when we play Singstar, there's a little whisper in my head reminding me I'll never sound like Molly. I hoped we wouldn't have to sing at EDDDA unless we wanted to – Liam would probably put it online to embarrass me.

"Not everyone will be singers," Molly said, as though reading my mind. "Don't forget there's a stage-management course too."

The one Nathan had been going to do, I remembered, before his plans had changed. For a second, I wondered where he was – would he have landed yet? Then Mrs Papadopoulos stopped the car and glanced back at us with a cheerful smile. "We're here, girls."

I thought about pretending I'd developed a mysterious allergy to performing and getting Molly's mum to take me back home but Molly and Shenice were excited to the max and I didn't want to crash their moods. Besides, I couldn't bear the thought of Liam's smugness if I gave up now, not to mention all the trouble Mum had gone to just to get me here. Gritting my teeth, I got out of the car.

The building was so modern it made St Jude's look like it belonged in the Stone Age. Huge glass windows towered over us into a triangular roof. Inside, I could see a lot of pale wood and even more glass. If the Egyptians had known how to make windows, this is what the pyramids would have looked like. I half expected Tutankha-wotsit to appear holding a clipboard.

There were around forty kids waiting outside, ranging from a few years younger than me to about fourteen or fifteen. I recognized a handful from school, including – GROAN – Imani Willis, my least favourite classmate. She had a bit of a thing for Nathan and was the girl most likely to push me off the stage if she got the chance. Molly, Shenice and I huddled together under our umbrellas, trying to pick out who the stars of the future might be. Some of the girls wore neon leg warmers and had their hair scraped into tight little buns — it didn't take EINSTEIN to work out they must be dancers. Another group seemed to be trying to recreate PITCH PERFECT in the car park, although judging from the look on Molly's face some of the notes they were riffing were a long way from perfect. Everywhere I looked, I saw excited, confident faces. No one seemed anxious and unsure like me.

The doors opened and we were ushered inside.

"Surnames beginning A to M this way," called a woman, pointing to a table at one end of the huge glass-covered entrance hall. "N to Z that way."

Shenice grabbed my hand and dragged me towards the first table, while Molly and her mum went to the opposite one. The queue hummed with excitement.

"I hear Miss Skelly used to be really famous," the girl in front of us was saying to her friend. "I think she was in PHANTOM OF THE OPERA when it first opened."

"Imagine that," the other girl breathed, lifting off her black trilby hat and clasping it to her chest. "I'd do ANYTHING to be a West End star."

I'd do anything not to make a fool of myself but it didn't seem like the right thing to say so I kept quiet.

When we reached the front, a man ticked us off on his list and we were given name badges and student passes to hang around our necks. I squinted down at mine – CASSIDY BOND: FUTURE STAR. Shenice clutched at my arm and held hers up so I could see it – SHENICE COLEMAN: TOMORROW'S TALENT.

"Did you get registered, girls?"
Mrs Papadopoulos said,
coming to stand next to us.
"Do you have everything
you need from the car?
Packed lunches?
Water bottles?"

We nodded, although what I actually needed was
a confidence transfusion. I'd have to hope that some of
Molly's poise rubbed off on me. The same woman who'd
directed us to the tables began to wave her arms,
ushering us further inside. "Once you've registered,
please make your way into Dance Studio One for
introductions. All students to DS1, please."

Molly's mum smiled. "Sounds like it's show time.
Let me know what time you need to be picked up later,
Molly."

She waved us goodbye and I thought about clinging onto her leg like a toddler on their first day at nursery, but it was much too late for that. As we followed the crowd, Shenice leaned towards Molly. "What does your student pass say?"

She held it up, grinning. MOLLY PAPADOPOULOS – NEXT BIG THING. It was probably about right, I decided, as we filed into the dance studio. If Molly was a stick of rock she'd have STAR running through her middle.

The dance studio was one of the most mind-melting places I've ever been. It was huge for a start, with a smooth wooden floor and spotlights in the ceiling. All four walls were covered by floor-to-ceiling mirrors, which made the room seem even bigger. Instead of forty or so students, there was now an enormous army of us, reflected over and over again. The air was filled with excited chatter, until we were interrupted by a booming voice.

"Good morning," it said, bouncing off the mirrors and into our ears like an extremely well-spoken sledgehammer. "Welcome to EDDDA, where your transformation from caterpillar to butterfly begins!"

CHAPTER FOUR

Everyone turned to stare as a tall, super-thin woman about the same age as my nan swept into the middle of the room. The buzz of excitement died as she peered haughtily around and it felt as though every single one of us was holding our breath.

"My name is Miss Skelly and I am your principal."

Molly leaned towards Shenice and me. "THAT is how you make an entrance," she whispered in an awed tone.

She had a point – Miss Skelly definitely had our attention. Even though a lot of the people there DRESSED TO IMPRESS, she stood out. It wasn't just her outfit, although that was pretty amazing – she carried an ebony-black walking cane with a huge amber globe on the top, and her curly grey hair was mostly covered by a purple turban that was twice as big as her head. No, it was her overall attitude, like she was a queen and we were – I don't know – peasants or something. Then there was her voice, which sounded really deep and husky, like my mum did when she had a chest infection a few months ago but a lot more COMMANDING.

To be completely honest, Miss Skelly is one of the

weirdest people I'd ever seen, except that weird isn't quite the right word. She's ECCENTRIC, which is basically the same as BATFLAP CRAZY but for some reason everyone pretends that it's fine. She sounds VAIR posh, too. I think she might even out-queen the Queen, except that she finished the occasional sentence with the word "daaaaaarling". But even that wasn't the funniest thing about Miss Skelly. No, the funniest thing was the stuff she came out with.

"Pee. Em. Aiee," she barked at us as we clustered around the edges of the dance studio. Tapping her cane on the polished floor, she fixed us with a piercing glare. "Positive Mental Attitude, darling. That's what you need to succeed in the theatre."

She said the last word strangely, with the emphasis on the first two syllables: THE-ATE-ERR. Shenice and I exchanged a wide-eyed look but Molly was transfixed.

"The next four weeks will be hard," Miss Skelly went on, her eyes narrowing. "You will sweat, you will cry and you may even bleed, although we try to avoid that last one for health-and-safety reasons. And if you do not have a Pee Em Aiee, you will not survive this academy. I have no time for naysayers. I have no time for can't-dos. I am solely interested in Pee. Oh. Oh."

I frowned. Wait – had Miss Skelly really just said she was only interested in...POO? Muffled giggles broke out around me and I felt Shenice grip my arm hard as I tried not to snort with laughter.

"Positive Outcomes Only," Miss Skelly barked and the laughter stopped instantly. "I expect nothing less than your best at all times. This is not a school for slackers – if you intend to give anything less than 110 per cent, you should leave now. Because the stage is an unforgiving mistress and a paying audience is even harder to please. But neither are as demanding as me."

I glanced around. One or two people were shifting uncomfortably and a few looked downright TERRIFIED, making me wonder if they were thinking what I was thinking – whether we could make it to the door before that vicious-looking cane could trip us up. But Molly was drinking it all in, her face shining as she stared at the principal.

Miss Skelly's voice softened a bit. "I promise that each and every one of you has the potential to burn brightly. But first, you must light the spark. And now I shall hand over to our director, Mr Pertwee, who will explain what the next four weeks hold."

There were a few sniggers at the mention of Mr Pertwee's name. He looked reassuringly normal as he took his place beside Miss Skelly. "Hi, guys. Firstly, can I say how great it is to meet you all? I'm really looking forward to working with you. And secondly, we're not at school so you can call me Nick."

Nick went on to explain how the academy would work.
We started at eight-thirty every morning – cue groans
and grumbles from us – and finished at five o'clock in the
evening. For the first week, we'd be getting to know each
other, learning how to unleash our inner performer and
working through the music for a big musical production
at the end of
the course.

"Told you so," Molly mouthed and I nodded, although
I couldn't help wondering if I even had an inner
performer.

"This Friday there will be auditions for anyone
who wants a speaking, singing or dancing role," Nick
went on, "and then it's non-stop rehearsals to whip
your performances into shape ready for the one-night-
only show."

It sounded stomach-churning but judging from the

excited babbling all around me, I was the only person who thought so. A couple of people seemed ready to do their audition right there and then.

"Being in the limelight is not for everyone," Nick said, finishing up. "For those of you who prefer to stay backstage, we'll be looking for costume designers and props managers as well as stagehands. In fact, there's a stage-management course running right next door which you can transfer over to at any time. They'll be helping to produce our set for the performance."

Maybe it would be best all round if I switched course now, I thought as I took in all the eager faces around me. Liam was right — I wasn't really a performer and I definitely wasn't the Next Big Thing like Molly. But then I remembered his taunting expression and I clenched my hands into fists. I wouldn't let him spoil this for me. I WOULDN'T.

Molly had been fidgeting all the way through Nick's speech and now she stuck her hand up in the air.

"Yes?" he said.

"What show are we doing?" she asked.

I knew she was hoping for **WICKED** – she'd been banging on about it for weeks and telling us what a great Glinda she'd make.

He smiled. "You're keen. I like that. I'm pleased to announce that this year's production will be **BUGSY MALONE**."

Everyone started talking at once. A few people burst into applause and the Pitch Perfect gang started to sing again.

"**BUGS ALONE**?" Shenice said, looking puzzled. "What's it about – ants?"

"That's **A BUG'S LIFE**," I said but I felt just as confused as she did. I'd never heard of **BUGSY MALONE** and while I was new to the acting game, surely that was a bad sign? Molly, on the other hand, looked like she might explode with excitement.

"It is such an amazing show," she said, her eyes bright. "Auntie Eleni took me to see it in London and we loved it. We've got it on DVD too."

"What's it about?" I asked, really hoping she wasn't about to say spiders.

She grinned. "It's a gangster story set in 1920s New York. It's got a car chase, a love triangle, and loads of people get shot. It's brilliant."

Shenice and I exchanged looks. "It doesn't sound very green," Shen said. "In fact, it sounds a bit violent. I don't think my mum will like it."

"But I haven't explained the best bit," Molly said. "The cars are all pedal-powered and the guns fire this foam stuff instead of bullets so no one really dies. Well, apart from Knuckles. But trust me, it's aces. We're going to have so much fun!"

"Settle down, everyone," Nick said, raising his hands. "You'll get copies of the script later on today. But for now, I'd like you to form a big circle because we've got an emergency. You're all about to die!"

If he meant of embarrassment I was WAY ahead of him.

"Relax," Molly said, grinning at me. "He probably means we're going to play Wink Murder."

Sometimes it's not so bad having a BFF who's a drama know-it-all, because Wink Murder was exactly what Nick had in mind. One person was elected the detective and left the room while we agreed who the killer would be. Then the detective came back in and the murderer worked their way around the circle, picking us off one by one with a sneaky wink.

Needless to say, in a room full of drama wannabes, the deaths got OTT really fast. Molly clutched at her chest, staggered backwards and let out a heart-rending moan as she dropped to the ground. Shenice, on the other hand, stood there like a lamp post until Molly reached up from the grave to tug her down. When it was my turn, I opted for strangulation, choking as I fell first to my knees and then to the floor. Before I closed my eyes, I saw Miss Skelly watching me. She whispered something to Nick and he stared at me too. Maybe I'd overdone it, I thought, as the boy next to me screamed as though he'd been shot. By the time the detective caught the murderer mid-wink, the body count was higher than a game of ZOMBIE CULL.

"Well done, everyone," Nick called. "Some gruesome

and dramatic deaths there. Get back in the circle and we're going to play another game."

This time we had to catch a ball and say our name, which was easy enough. But then we had to add in the name of the person who'd thrown us the ball and that's when it got tricky. My head was whirling from all the different names – the dancer in the hot-pink leg warmers was called Tucker, the girl in the trilby $\longrightarrow$ hat from the queue was Suzuma, and there was a dark-haired boy of around our age called Harry, who looked like he'd stepped straight out of a boy band. But the truth was I could barely remember my own name after a while. I'm pretty sure I called one of the girls Peter but I think I got away with it.

"Good work," Nick said eventually. "Now split into pairs for some role-play work."

Oh no. That is definitely the worst thing about having two besties — if you have to form a pair for anything, one of you is always going to be left out. We stared at each other in panic, none of us wanting to volunteer for the embarrassment of going it alone on our first day. Nick bustled past us. "Come on, girls, sort it out."

When none of us moved, he sighed and tapped Molly on the shoulder. "Okay, how about you work with Harry over here?"

Biting her lip, Molly nodded and followed Nick over to Boy-Band-Boy.

"I don't know why she's looking so miserable," Shenice muttered under her breath. "He's a lot cuter than you are."

"Rude," I sniffed, but I glanced over at Molly's

partner with renewed interest. I had to admit Shenice was right – he was pretty cute. I watched as he smiled at Molly and began chatting like he'd known her for ever.

Nick cleared his throat and everyone quietened down. "One of you is going to play the parent and the other is going to play a child with a mysterious illness. The parent has to try to catch the child fibbing about how sick they are. You have two minutes starting now!"

Shenice is the world's worst liar and it didn't take me long to catch her out. We spent the rest of the time pretending to act while really studying Molly and Harry. It soon became obvious they were on a mission to outdo each other.

"Wow," Shenice said, her expression even more admiring. "He's really good."

He was, but Molly was totally holding her own and we

weren't the only ones who noticed – Miss Skelly was hovering nearby, listening in. Then Nick told us to swap roles and I tried my hardest to convince Shen that I was suffering from a terrible disease that made my eyes cross. She was too busy laughing to catch me out and I declared myself the winner at the end. And then I realized something amazing: all my nerves had faded away and I was actually enjoying myself.

"You know, this isn't so bad," I told Shenice as Nick made us form a big circle again. "Liam almost had me convinced I'd do something stupid within seconds but so far, so good."

"One last exercise before we give out the scripts," Nick told us. "One by one you have to stand up and share an interesting fact about yourself. If you can't think of a fact, you can make something up and we'll try to guess whether it's true. For example, my name is Nick and I am married to Beyoncé."

Everyone laughed. "You wish!" someone shouted.

Nick held up his hands. "Okay, you got me. Let's start over here."

He pointed to a boy on the opposite side of the circle. "My name is Nitheran and I am a chess champion."

That was a tough one – he totally looked like he could be king of the most boring game known to mankind.

"True?" the girl next to him said and he nodded, looking pretty proud of himself.

We worked our way around the circle. Harry made everyone laugh by revealing he'd rugby-tackled one of Snow White's dwarfs in Disneyland when he was six. When it got to Molly, my stomach began to flip-flop with nerves. What was I going to say? "Hello, I'm Cassidy and my dog has a thing about my knickers"? Or "Hello, I'm Cassidy and my dad thinks he's Elvis"? Hmmm, maybe not either of those. Molly didn't have the same problem, though.

"My name is Molly," she said, her voice ringing with confidence, "and I once played keepy-uppy with David Beckham."

Both Shenice and I knew this was true – he'd been opening the new sports stadium in Windsor and Molly had only been around four or five at the time – so we kept quiet. But I knew looking at Molly's ringlets and heart-shaped face that hardly anyone would believe she'd played football with such a superstar.

"No way!" one boy shouted and his mates jeered in agreement.

Most of the other kids looked doubtful but

Harry grinned. "I reckon that happened."

Molly nodded and sat down. Shenice was next but she didn't stand up. I glanced at her to see she was staring at Harry with a dreamy expression on her face. Uh oh...

"Shen," I nudged her as discreetly as I could. "Shen, it's your turn."

Her eyes widened suddenly and her cheeks went pink. She stood up. "Um...my name is Shenice and I — erm — I..."

Everyone waited. The silence got louder and louder. Just say anything, I thought to myself, cringing on her behalf. Tell them you're a lion tamer. Say your dad is President of the United States. **ANYTHING.**

When we reached 9.5 on the ——> SHAME-O-METER, I couldn't bear it any more and jumped to my feet,

intending to rescue Shenice. But the movement seemed to jolt her from her trance. She stared at me with panicky eyes for a heartbeat, then reached out and grabbed my arm. "I'm Shenice and this is Cassidy and we're starring in the West End production of MATILDA this September."

Willing my face not to turn red, I tried to look like a CHILD PRODIGY when actually all I wanted to do was goggle at Shenice. Where had that come from? One minute she was a total SPACE CADET and the next she sounded so confident that even I half believed her. And from the looks of things, our fellow students were struggling to work out whether it was fact or fib too. Some of them were watching us with narrowed eyes, others were arguing among themselves, but not even the kids who went to St Jude's seemed to know whether we were telling the truth.

Harry was watching Shenice, his expression thoughtful. "You'd make an amazing Lavender," he told her, before turning his gaze on me. "And you...maybe Hortensia?"

Well, this was AWKWARD – Harry obviously believed we were capable of winning big roles in a huge musical and now Shenice had to admit that she'd lied. It wasn't the best way to create a first impression. Then again, the whole point of the game was to fool people.

"Nope," I said, shaking my head. "I'm playing Bruce Bogtrotter, actually."

Shenice threw me a grateful look. "And I'm playing his cake."

Everyone laughed, Harry included and the next person stood up to speak. Harry leaned past Molly to tap Shenice on the shoulder. "I still think you'd be a brilliant Lavender."

Shenice blushed. "Thanks."

I swear something flashed between them then, just like it does in the movies when boy meets girl. Molly must have caught it too because she winked at me over the top of Shen's head. At least I think that's what she was getting at — she might have been trying to murder me, I suppose. But whatever she meant, it's safe to say that Shenice seems wild about Harry.

It was kind of a buzz making everyone laugh. Maybe I won't swap courses just yet.

Eton Dorney Dance and Drama Academy
Where the Stars of Tomorrow Start Shining!

AUDITION INSTRUCTIONS

At EDDDA, we encourage EVERYONE to audition for a role. You never know what you can do until you try! Below, you'll find a list of the main speaking roles but there are many other parts to be cast too, so if you aren't successful in your audition for a bigger part, we may cast you in a smaller role.

Auditions will be held on Friday, with the results being announced on Monday.

Good luck!

Miss Skelly and Mr Pertwee

Principal Roles

BUGSY MALONE – the main man, a boxing scout getting ready for the big time

BLOUSEY BROWN – a smart and sassy singer who dreams of Hollywood

FAT SAM – a mobster crime boss and speakeasy owner

TALLULAH – a beautiful singer, Fat Sam's girl with a soft spot for Bugsy

DANDY DAN – a rival gangster who outsmarts Fat Sam at every turn

FIZZY – tap-dancing caretaker of Fat Sam's Speakeasy, dancing role

LENA MARELLI – a loud, show-off theatre performer

FAT SAM'S HOODLUMS – Knuckles, Snake Eyes, Ritzy, Roxy Robinson, Shade Down Louis

FAT SAM'S SPEAKEASY GIRLs – Bangles, Velma, Loretta, Dotty, Tillie

DANDY DAN'S GANG – Louella, Bronz Charlie, Benny Lee, Yonkers Charlie, Doodle

Audition Songs

Please choose ONE song only:

GIRLS

"Ordinary Fool" (sung by Blousey)
"My Name is Tallulah" (sung by Tallulah)
"Bugsy Malone" (sung by the Speakeasy Girls)

BOYS

"Down and Out" (sung by Bugsy)
"Bad Guys" (sung by Fat Sam's Hoodlums)
"Tomorrow" (sung by Fizzy)

CHAPTER FIVE

The rest of the day whizzed by in a blur of songs and acting lessons. I was a bit nervous when Nick announced he was going to give each of us a SCORE but it turns out that's just a fancy word for the music to go with the show. And there was a minor panic when Miss Skelly told us we had to PROJECT but that just means talk loudly so that the audience can hear. The only homework we were given was to watch the film version of BUGSY MALONE, so Molly phoned her mum to arrange an emergency sleepover that night and we piled into her bedroom, brimming over with popcorn and excitement.

Molly is so **LUCKY**. She's an only child for a start, so there are no annoying brothers or sisters to compete for her parents' attention. The rest of her family is huge — I don't think even she knows how many cousins she has but she gets loads of presents at Christmas and on her birthday. She's been a bridesmaid nine times already and is always going back to Greece for family weddings. The only bridesmaid-potential in my family is if Uncle Ian proposes to Auntie Jane but Dad says there is more chance of the Pope getting married than of Uncle Ian popping the question. Does the Pope even have a girlfriend?

Anyway, Molly's house is practically the size of **WINDSOR CASTLE** but without the parapets and you don't have to climb

over a mountain of baby equipment to get past the front door. She's got a flat-screen TV on the wall of her bedroom and the latest games console plugged into it and her mum is allergic to dogs so I can't imagine that anyone has ever puked grass-filled slime on her rose-covered duvet cover. I could probably live in her wardrobe and she would never notice. In fact, the only thing Molly's room has in common with mine is THE DROIDS posters on the wall and even those have mostly been replaced by WOLF BRETHREN photos now, which just proves my theory that she is also a teensy bit insane. Did I mention that Molly is the LUCKIEST GIRL ALIVE?

So we watched BUGSY MALONE and sat with our scores open to sing along to the songs. Fat Sam has some great insults and I made a mental note to call Liam a DUMB SALAMI as soon as I could. I couldn't wait to see how Miss Skelly planned to transform the stage into FAT SAM'S GRAND SLAM SPEAKEASY – she'd need a bar and tables and chairs, at least, plus a huge dollop of gangster glamour. And how would she manage the splurge guns? Foam? Custard, maybe?

"Which part are you going to audition for?" I asked Molly when the end credits started to roll. "Blousey or Tallulah?"

She stared up at the ceiling. "I don't know. Tallulah's song is better than Blousey's, but Blousey does get Bugsy at the end. Maybe I'll see what Miss Skelly suggests."

Molly came third in the ST JUDE'S HAS GOT TALENT contest the school held last year and I'm pretty sure she'll be a professional singer some day, so it was no surprise she had her eye on one of the big roles.

What I wasn't ready for was the determined gleam that suddenly appeared in Shenice's eye. "I think I'm going to go for Tallulah."

Molly and I stared at her in astonishment. "Okay,"
I demanded in a shocked voice, "who are you and what
have you done with Shenice?"

She frowned at me. "Why? Don't you think I can
do it?"

My BFF loyalty kicked in.
"Of course I do," I gushed.
"You'd be a great Tallulah.
It's just...well, it's a pretty
big part and your last big role
was the angel in the school ———▶
nativity play in Year Three.
We're just a bit surprised, that's all."

Molly nodded. "Yeah, there'll be a lot of girls
auditioning for Tallulah. Competition will be fierce." She
paused and I got the feeling she was picking her words
with great care. "Wouldn't you rather go for something a

bit smaller? What about one of Fat Sam's dancers –
Bangles is a great role? Or Lena Marelli, the showgirl who
interrupts Blousey's first audition. She's a great character
and a real scene stealer."

"No," Shenice said with a stubborn shake of her head.
"It's got to be Tallulah. You saw the film – whoever plays
her gets to kiss Bugsy."

She'd lost me – what did that have to do with
anything? Molly looked just as confused. Picking up my
script, I flicked through it until I found the scene she
meant, the one where Tallulah kisses Bugsy on the
forehead to make Blousey jealous. And then I noticed the
dreamy look in Shen's eyes, the same look she'd had when
she'd been staring at Harry pretty much the whole day,
and the penny dropped: in her head, Shenice had already
cast herself as the kisser and Harry as the kissed.

"Oh..." I said. "Got you."

"OH!" Molly exclaimed, her eyes on the script. "I get it too."

Shenice's expression clouded over as though she'd suddenly been hit by the DOUBT FAIRIES. "Unless...you don't think I'm good enough?"

I thought of all the times Molly and Shenice had encouraged me — like when I'd been sure that Nathan never wanted to speak to me again or when I'd worried I wasn't clever enough for the quiz team. How would I have felt if they'd been negative instead of super-supportive? And then I remembered Miss Skelly's Pee Em Aiee talk. Maybe Shenice had the right idea after all — to step out of her comfort zone and reach for her dreams. Maybe all she needed was a chance to shine. My eyes met Molly's and she smiled.

"Of course you're good enough," Molly said. "And big dreams are much better than small ones."

"She's right," I agreed, thinking of a poster I'd seen once. "If you shoot for the moon you might land among the stars."

Shenice looked a little bit happier. "That's what I thought. So – uh – have you got any tips, Molly?"

"Loads!" Molly said, her voice bubbly with enthusiasm. "Why don't we all learn the song and we can help each other?"

It was a sweet idea but I was fairly sure there was NOTHING I could teach Molly about singing. Shenice looked down. "Oh. I was kind of hoping you wouldn't audition for her too. Didn't you say Blousey was a better role?"

EEK. This was a huge favour, one I would never have dared to ask. Molly is a born performer and it seemed really unfair of Shenice to ask her to give up Tallulah.

Then again, I wouldn't want to audition against Molly –
she was bound to have her pick of the girls' roles. I
glanced back and forth between them, my stomach tense.
Molly's face had gone all pink and I thought she might be
about to cry. Then she sucked in a deep breath. "Okay.
I'll audition for Blousey."

Shenice squealed and threw herself across the room
to hug Molly. I piled on too and we tumbled into a big
giggling heap. That's the great thing about Molly – she
might be used to being the star of the show most of the
time but she hasn't let it go to her head – she'd never
ditch a BFF for a few minutes of fame.

Molly also loves being in charge and sure
enough about ten seconds later, she pushed her
way out of the huddle and picked up her pen
like it was a conductor's baton.

"There's an old saying in show business: 'Fame costs'

and you have to work your butt off if you want to succeed," she said, pointing the pen at Shenice. "Miss Skelly wants sweat and tears and Pee Oh Oh."

I couldn't help myself – I sniggered. Molly narrowed her eyes. "Don't think I'm letting you off the hook, Cassie. Who are you auditioning for?"

I froze. I hadn't really planned to audition at all – the idea of getting up onstage on my own and singing seemed like a disaster waiting to happen. "Er...no one?"

She raised her eyebrows. "I thought acting was going to be your thing? Didn't she say that, Shenice?"

Shen threw me a sympathetic look but she nodded. "Sorry, Cass, you did say that."

"Don't let Liam put you off," Molly said, leaning forward. I'd told them about his comments last night.

"Performing often runs in families, look at all the big acting dynasties there are. I bet Liam's just scared you'll be better than him."

Was I dreaming or had Molly just said something almost critical about Liam?

"But I'd be intimidated too, if I had a brother who was so awesomely talented," she went on, spoiling the moment a bit. "What you need to do is focus on your own performance and forget Liam even exists."

"Shouldn't be too hard," I muttered. I spent a large part of every day trying to pretend Liam didn't exist.

Molly was busy studying the audition sheet. "It looks as though you can both sing Tallulah's song even though you're not auditioning for that role, Cassidy." She hesitated. "You're not, are you?"

Shenice looked up from her score.

"Not a chance," I replied. "I'd rather sit through double maths every day for a year."

Blinking with relief, Molly forwarded the DVD until it was at the start of Tallulah's song. "Okay, sometimes my singing teacher makes me do a visualization exercise. Basically, you imagine yourself getting the part you want and create a picture in your mind."

I glanced at the audition sheet – which role was the right one for me? One of the Speakeasy Girls? Or the one Molly had suggested to Shenice – Lena Marelli?

"See yourself striding onto the stage like you own it," Molly said, in a funny, sing-song voice. "You're going to absolutely smash this audition. You're ready. You were BORN ready."

Shen had closed her eyes so I copied her and tried to imagine myself auditioning in front of Miss Skelly. She was smiling and clapping. Now she was blowing me kisses and someone was throwing roses.

"Summon up your Pee Em Aiee," Molly urged. "Visualize that Pee Oh Oh. And when you can see it, reach out and grab it."

URGH, not without a pooper scooper. And just like that, my vision vanished. I heard Shenice groan and I knew the same thing had happened to her.

Molly stared at us in bewilderment, completely unaware of what she'd just said. Honestly, she might be a great singer but sometimes you can really tell she's never had a pet.

Want to hear something strange? Molly's weird
visualization trick actually works! I woke up this
morning feeling much more confident. It could be the
HOURS of rehearsal Molly made us do last night – I feel
like MY NAME IS TALLULAH will be rattling round my
head FOR EVER – but it was totally worth it. Shenice
can sing the whole song without the help of the DVD now
and I can mumble along too, although the notes aren't
always in the right order. Molly is a really strict teacher
– I think she would have made us carry on all night
if her mum hadn't complained we were drowning out
the TV.

So maybe Molly is onto something when she says
imagining success really helps us to BECOME a success.
Or maybe my inner performer is starting to come out
from wherever she's been hiding. Whatever the reason,
I'm beginning to think I might just belong at EDDDA
after all. Which can only be a good thing, since Shenice
was so keen to go that she woke us up at six o'clock this

morning. PMAs are much harder to come by when
someone is bouncing on your feet.

I think I'm going to audition for the part of Lena
the showgirl. It's not a big role but she's funny and
I think maybe I can pull it off. Even Oscar winners have
to start somewhere.

To act, you must be a chameleon.

You must know yourself so well that you can change everything you are, become someone else. You must believe that you are your character and every action and reaction must be what they would do. In short, you will no longer be YOU.

In the space below, list the obstacles that are preventing you from becoming one with your character:

✳ LIAM – so desperate to keep his title as THE MUSICAL ONE that he has started shouting "It's a NO from me!" every time he hears me singing.

✳ MY BFFs – Molly is brilliant OF COURSE and Shenice is getting better every day – Nick gave her a round of applause in one of our workshops this week. I am not jealous of them but I really wish some of their sparkle would rub off on me. Just a little bit.

✱ NERVES – I am pretty nervous about auditioning, in spite of my PMA. Molly says that nerves give you an edge but the way I feel right now they are more likely to tip me over it.

✱ PRESSURE – knowing I was given a bursary to be at EDDDA isn't helping with my nerves. What if Miss Skelly decides I am not good enough and asks for a refund? I'm not sure I want acting to be my THING after all. It's not as easy as it looks.

CHAPTER SIX

I have discovered a fundamental flaw in my plan to conquer the world of show business.

I CANNOT SING.

I mean, of course I can sing, everyone can — you just open your mouth and noise comes out. And I can even do it in tune most of the time, as proved by my eighty per cent accuracy rating on Singstar. But it turns out that's a lot different to singing solo in front of people who are not

Molly and Shenice, without a backing track. Whenever we have to sing in our workshops, I get all nervous and my voice shrivels away into a SQUEAKY WHISPER that even a MOUSE would struggle to hear. I am a little bit annoyed with Molly for making it all look so easy because it turns out that performing is HARD. The auditions are tomorrow morning and I am seriously considering hiding under my bed and faking a ransom note. To think people do this for fun. Why? WHY?

Molly is an old hand at auditions and she says they are the WORST THING EVER. She told Shenice and me that the actual performing part is much easier but she doesn't seem in the least bit nervous. Even Shenice seems to have the nerves under control, although she gets totally flustered around Harry, and I know she's pinned her entire future happiness on playing Tallulah, which is a pretty big part compared to Lena. So why am I the only one whose PMA seems to have run away?

Dad came in to see me at bedtime. "How are you feeling?"

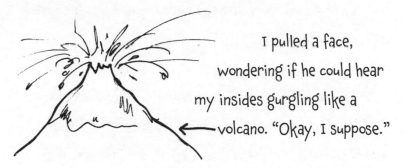

I pulled a face, wondering if he could hear my insides gurgling like a volcano. "Okay, I suppose."

He smiled. "Let me guess – you're worried if you open your mouth too wide all your dinner will come out, right?"

I nodded. Let's face it, it wouldn't be the first time my stomach has let me down at the critical moment. I'd puked on Nathan's feet once – not my finest moment.

"You wouldn't mind if I didn't audition, would you?" I asked.

"Me?" he said, looking surprised. "It's nothing to do with me. This is only your first show after all and there's

97

a lot of fun to be had from staying in the chorus."

A whoosh of relief washed over me and I sagged back against my pillow.

"But here's the thing," Dad went on. "How are you going to feel on Monday morning when they post the audition results on the wall and everyone is buzzing about which role they're going to be playing? What if Molly and Shenice get speaking parts and you're left behind in the chorus? Will you be glad for them or will you wish you'd taken the risk and auditioned?"

I tried to imagine the scene. Molly would get Blousey, I was sure of that. I'd seen Nick's face during the audition workshops and he seemed really pleased with how she'd sung already. Harry was practically guaranteed Bugsy — the rumour was that he'd been offered a place at the Anna Contessa Stage School in London and was due to start in September. Imani Willis had been boasting all week about

how she was the perfect Tallulah but Shenice's crush on
Harry had reached EPIC proportions and had inspired her
to work even harder. I didn't think I'd ever seen her so
determined, not even when she was training for the
Berkshire Junior Swimming Trials, and I had everything
crossed that she could snatch Tallulah from underneath
Imani's overconfident nose.

I pictured the excitement and hubbub as they
swarmed around the list on the wall. Then I imagined
myself standing back, not really part of the group.
Without an audition there would be no danger of being
crushed by disappointment if I didn't get the part
I wanted, but there was also no chance of that mega-
whooping happiness if I did.

"I don't know," I said. "What would you do?"

"Blow their minds with Elvis," he said, grinning.

"Dad," I groaned. "Be serious."

"Okay," he said. "I would audition. You're bound to
feel a bit sick but that's normal. And if you don't get the
part you'll end up in the chorus, where you would have
been if you hadn't tried. Would that be so terrible?"

"No," I replied, trying not to visualize myself
throwing up on the audition panel.

"Right. And what's the best that
could happen? You get the part and
knock Miss Skelly's socks off." ⟶

I doubt Miss Skelly wears socks – she's too
extraordinary for those. But Dad had a point. I'd never
know if acting was my big talent if I didn't take the risk.
"Maybe you're right."

He gave me a hug. "I know I'm right. And if nothing

else, imagine how furious Liam will be when you prove that you've got the talent for performing too."

And that is possibly the most genius idea I have ever heard in my life. When I get up onstage tomorrow, I am going to mentally project Liam's cross face onto the faces of the audition panel members. If that doesn't spur me on to performing success, nothing will.

Shenice and her mum arrived dead on time, in spite of my last-minute wish for a freak solar flare to bubble the road surface and cause traffic chaos. Mum gave me a fierce hug on my way out of the door and Ethel licked my nose, which I took to mean "good luck", but none of it could stop my stomach from squirming. By the time we'd arrived at EDDDA, I was a complete WRECK. What in the name of Wham bars made me think I could do this?

The auditions were being held in the theatre itself,

which meant we'd be performing on the stage. Dance Studio One was packed with hopefuls and a couple of teachers. Some students were sitting down, staring at their scripts and fervently whispering the words. Others were listening to headphones and a few were stood up and staring into space, presumably channelling their PMA. Either that or they were trying to get a grip on their blind panic like me. I spotted Harry in a corner, looking pretty chilled out considering I knew he was going for the lead role. Imani kept trying to catch his eye but he kept his head down, although I'm pretty sure I saw him wink at Shen once.

Every now and then, the door would open and a name would be called. The lucky victim would go, usually with calls of support and cheering, and we wouldn't see them again. Well, until lunchtime, anyway.

Molly and Shenice had just decided to slip off to the toilets for one final rehearsal when Molly's name was called. Looking calm and composed, she followed one of the teachers out of the room. The minutes ticked by. No one said much and, if they did talk, they mostly whispered. It was like a really rubbish version of THE HUNGER GAMES, where nobody was hungry and without any actual fighting. At least I hoped there wasn't — maybe that was what happened if they couldn't decide who to give a part to. Anyway, I had everything crossed for Molly, although I was pretty sure she'd be knocking it out of the park. Then the door opened and it was someone else's turn. Shenice whipped out her phone, typing fast. I leaned over her shoulder to read.

How did it go? X

It felt like ages before the screen lit up with a reply, during which a zillion possibilities whizzed through my mind — she'd totally flopped and didn't know how to tell us...her phone battery had mysteriously died...it really WAS The Hunger Games and she'd lost...

OK. Think I heard Miss Skelly sniffling but she might just have hay fever.
Break a leg! X

Break a leg? What kind of thing was that for a so-called best friend to wish on someone just before an audition? I opened my mouth to tell Shen that Molly had CHANGED but the door opened again before I could speak.

"Shenice Coleman?"

Shen closed her eyes for a second and then threw me a worried look as she stood up. "Good luck!" I said, holding up my tightly crossed fingers. "I've even got my eyes crossed – look!"

She smiled faintly and that's when I knew how nervous she really was, because normally she cannot resist my cross-eyed craziness. Harry gave her the thumbs up as she left, which I hope made up for the evil eye Imani fired at her back. I stared down at my script while I waited, but they blurred in front of my eyes.

This time the waiting was even harder, because I was on my own and I knew how much Shenice wanted to play Tallulah. The moment the next victim was called, I was on my phone.

WELL? X

The clock on the wall ticked. Someone made the kind of smell that made me look around for Liam. And finally – FINALLY – my phone buzzed.

I dunno – not bad? You can't see a thing from the stage. Good luck! X

Imani Willis went next and I spent a happy few minutes visualizing her tripping over her own feet and landing in the orchestra pit before realizing that it probably wasn't very good karma. My nerves were really kicking in now and I was starting to wonder if I could just pretend that I'd auditioned to Molly and Shenice. No one would judge me if I got up and walked out, would they? I could say I was going to the loo...

"Cassidy Bond?" a voice called.

AARGH – too late. I looked up to see Liz, one of the drama teachers, smiling at me. Lurching to my feet, I fixed my gaze on the floor as I walked to the door. "Break a leg!" I heard someone – Harry? – shout as I left. First Molly and now Harry – what IS with this leg-breaking stuff? They need to keep an eye out for karma too.

The wings of the stage were shadowy but I could just about make out dark curtains hanging in front of me.

"Stand centre stage, take a deep breath and tell them your name," Liz whispered as she pushed me towards the

gap in the curtains. "You're going
to be fine."

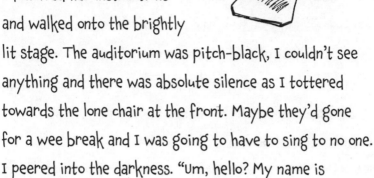

My legs wobbled as
I followed her instructions
and walked onto the brightly
lit stage. The auditorium was pitch-black, I couldn't see
anything and there was absolute silence as I tottered
towards the lone chair at the front. Maybe they'd gone
for a wee break and I was going to have to sing to no one.
I peered into the darkness. "Um, hello? My name is
Cassidy Bond and I'm auditioning for Lena Marelli."

There was a faint rustling of paper and then I heard
Nick's voice. "Okay, Cassidy, ready when you are."

The music began and my knees began to shake.
In fact, my whole body was trembling and I was sure
they must be able to hear the hammering of my heart.
"My name is Tallulah..."

The first note came out as more of a squawk and I could just imagine Miss Skelly's disapproving expression. I stared straight ahead, doing my best to follow the music and willed my heart to slow down. Any minute now they'll yell "CUT!" I thought, just like the scene in the film version of BUGSY where they're auditioning acts who really suck. But nobody interrupted and as the song went on, I felt a bit better. By the time I got to the final notes, it didn't sound bad. Not great but nowhere near as MOUSELIKE as I'd feared I would be.

"Thanks, Cassidy," Nick called. "Well done. Could you give us your Lena now, please?"

My mouth was drier than the Sahara but like a numpty I'd left my water bottle in the dance studio. Swallowing hard, I summoned up the scene from the film where Lena Marelli barges onto the stage, knocks Blousey out of the way and steals the show. Adopting a whiny American accent, I put my hands on my hips and thrust my chin in the air to deliver Lena's lines.

There was a moment of silence once I'd finished then Nick said, "Great job. Thank you, that's all for now."

I started to walk off but Miss Skelly's voice stopped me. "It says here you're away for a week at the start of August. Is that correct, darling?"

I cleared my throat. "Yes. We're going to Cornwall."

"Pity," Miss Skelly said briskly. "Next, please!"

I wondered what she meant all the way to the room where Molly and Shenice were waiting.

"Oh," Molly said after we'd shared our audition stories, her eyes wide. "It probably means she was thinking about giving you a part!"

Shenice started to squeal.

I frowned. "Was?"

Molly looked awkward. "Well, if there were two people in the running for a particular part, and one of them was going to miss a week of rehearsals, they'd probably give it to the person who was going to be there more. Sorry, Cassie."

My shoulders slumped in disappointment. Stupid holiday. I didn't even want to go and now it might get in the way of something I did want – a part in the show.

"I could be wrong," Molly said.

"No," I said, sighing, "I think you're right. But I wish they'd told me that before I put myself through auditioning."

Shenice shuddered. "Yeah, I thought I was going to faint from nerves at one point. I guess that's why they stopped me before I'd finished the song."

Molly and I exchanged looks. "They stopped you?" I said warily.

Shen nodded. "Yeah. I did the lines and then Nick shouted for me to stop about halfway through the song. Didn't they stop you?"

We shook our heads.

"I'm sure it doesn't mean anything, though," Molly said in a voice so chirpy I half expected her to sprout feathers. → "I expect you were so amazing that they knew you had the part there and then. Sometimes they just know someone is perfect for a role."

Shenice bit her lip, her eyes glittering with tears. "I bet it doesn't." She sighed and looked away. "It looks like you and me are going to be in the chorus, Cassie."

I can't believe we have to wait until Monday to find out the audition results. I don't know how we're supposed to survive a whole WEEKEND of not knowing — we'll be climbing the walls by Sunday night. What I really need is a way to get out of our stupid trip to Cornwall — something that will show Miss Skelly I have the commitment to play Lena.

Hmmm. Maybe I'll text Auntie Jane to ask about moving in with her. Mum said she used to do amateur dramatics when she was younger so she's bound to be on my side.

112

CHAPTER SEVEN

"Did you ask Auntie Jane if you can go and live with her?" Mum demanded the moment I got through the front door.

She looked cross. Even Joshua was being quiet, which meant either he was plotting something or he'd picked up on her mood and was keeping his head down.

"I might have done," I admitted, bending down to kiss Ethel in the baby bouncer. "Why, is it a problem?"

"A problem?" she repeated, glaring at me. "I'll say. What part of 'family holiday' do you not understand, Cassidy? It means we all go together. You don't opt out because you get a better offer."

"It's not that—" I began, but she was in full GRUMPY flow and didn't listen.

"Apart from anything else, what were you planning to do with Rolo? You know what he does to Uncle Ian's leg whenever he gets near him."

Rolo had the grace to look a bit embarrassed then but I knew from experience that it wouldn't be enough to stop him snuggling up to Uncle Ian the next time he saw him.

"I thought maybe you could take him," I said.

"He's your dog," Mum growled. "So you have to

be there to walk him, I'm afraid."

I sighed as my last hope flew out of the window.
"Okay, fine, I get the message."

She swung Joshua onto her other hip. "Good. What was
so important that you decided to try and ditch us,
anyway?"

I told her. When I'd finished, she looked a bit
less cross. "Oh. Well, I'm sorry you might miss out on
the part you want but I'm sure Miss Skelly understands.
If she wants to give you the role, she'll have to work
around you."

Which is probably true but not what I would call
helpful. This is what happens when your mother doesn't
understand you. I bet Angelina Jolie's kids don't have
this problem.

To: <u>BondGirl007</u>

From: <u>NathanC</u>

Hi Cassie!

Would you believe it is actually snowing in Tasmania? We even had a snowball fight this morning – which is really weird! I always thought it was hot all the time here.

How are things with you? You sounded a bit fed up – I'm sure your audition didn't sound like an out-of-tune violin. I bet you were really good. Fingers crossed you get the part you want – I wish I could come and see the show but we're due back a few days after the course finishes so there's no chance. Maybe someone will record it, though?

I'm well jealous of your holiday to Cornwall – cool beaches, great surf and you don't have to fly

10,000 miles to get there.
You'll have to take some
photos to show me when
you get back.

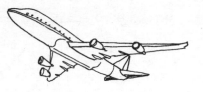

Anyway, I'd better go. I hope Rolo is behaving
himself. Give him a lump of cheese from me.

Nathan

You know when you hand in a piece of homework and part
of you wants to know what your teacher thought and
part of you doesn't? That's how I felt about the audition
results. I'd spent the whole weekend worrying and
fretting and by the time Monday morning rolled around,
I'd decided that I shouldn't even bother going back to
EDDDA. What I really needed was to discover a mysterious
spinning wheel in the attic which sent me into a deep
sleep lasting a hundred years, or at least until lunchtime,

but there is never
an evil fairy ⟶
around when you
need one.

    I SUPPOSE it
is all for the best – as
much as I'm sure there is no
hope for me, I do want to be there for Molly and Shenice,
even though Molly and I are secretly worried about
Shenice's short audition.

    The twins were already in their high chairs when I
went down for breakfast. Joshua was wearing most of a
banana and Ethel was using butter instead of wax to boost
her super-fine baby hair – neither seemed to have any
useful advice to offer me. Liam was nowhere to be seen
– still in bed, I assume. Dad says if sleeping was an
Olympic sport, Liam would win gold.

Shenice's mum arrived to pick me up at eight o'clock. The plan was that our parents would take it in turns to pick us up and drop us off but Mum obviously has her hands full with the twins and so Mrs Coleman and Mrs Papadopoulos are doing it most mornings. It is probably a good thing – between the baby seats, the buggies and the half-chewed breadsticks in our car, there's no space for anything else.

We didn't talk much in the car. I could practically taste the nerves, although Joshua shoved his grubby fingers into my mouth just before I left so it could have been mushed-up banana. In the corridor outside the dance studio, there was a big crowd clustered around the noticeboard. We looked at each other – this was it.

"Let's get it over with," Molly said.

Linking her arms through ours, she marched to the front of the crowd, dragging us with her.

I could hardly bear to look. Beside me, Molly let out an excited squeal and I squinted at the list. Sure enough, her name was there, right next to the words "Blousey Brown". Then I heard a sharp gasp on my other side and an even louder squeal. I looked down the list and saw Shenice had been cast as Tallulah!

"I can't believe it," she said, looking shocked and delighted all at the same time. "And look who got Bugsy!"

You didn't need to be a genius to guess it was Harry. Molly was jumping up and down with glee but my eyes were scanning the list, looking for my name. I found it halfway down: CASSIDY BOND — VELMA, FAT SAM'S SPEAKEASY GIRL.

Disappointed is not the word — it felt like someone had punched me in the stomach. Velma isn't even the best Speakeasy Girl part — Bangles has more lines than her. This was just a pat on the head — a "Well done for trying".

I wanted to cry. But I couldn't, not when my besties'
dreams had come true.

"Yay," I croaked, doing my very best to smile.
"You guys totally smashed it."

They stopped squealing.

"At least they gave you something," Shenice said,
sympathy dripping from her voice. "Velma has a line,
I think."

"It's only because you're missing a whole week of
rehearsals," Molly said. "They obviously wanted to give
you a bigger part but maybe they couldn't because you're
going away in two days' time."

I knew what they were saying made sense but it
didn't make me feel any better. And to make things
worse, I saw that Imani had been given the role of Lena

— the one I'd asked for on my audition form. It was all too unfair for words.

A proper BFF would be able to overcome her own disappointment and enjoy seeing how over the moon Molly and Shenice were, I told myself as I blinked back tears. They were going to be the stars of the show and I should be happy for them.

And don't get me wrong, I am pleased for them. But it's being swamped by the cold horrible feeling that I've failed. It doesn't matter how many times I force myself to smile, or how often I remind myself that I can still help them to sparkle, there is still a ragged empty hole where my heart should be. I gave 110 per cent and it wasn't enough.

Great. Now I'm a terrible friend as well as a rubbish actor.

What else can go wrong?

MISSING

One PMA, last seen in the Eton Dorney area.
If found, please return to Cassidy Bond.

CHAPTER EIGHT

If you've ever wondered what hell is like, let me tell you.
It is being stuck in a car for eight hours on a rainy
Wednesday with your family. Liam smells like only a
teenage boy can, Rolo has thrown up on my feet and the
twins have grizzled so much that my brain has turned
to slush. The traffic in Cornwall reminds me of a disaster
movie where everyone is trying to escape from the
monster-ravaged city at the same time – in other words,
totally gridlocked, although why everyone would head to
Newquay is a total mystery to me. And if Dad makes us

listen to **THE BEST OF ELVIS PRESLEY** one more time,
I may just leap out of the window and run for the cliffs.

The only good thing about this trip is that it is taking
me further and further away from **EDDDA**.

I haven't seen much of Molly and Shenice since
Monday – they've been off having private rehearsals with
the other principal stars of the show. To make up for
being the Worst Friend Ever I helped them run through
their lines on Monday evening – Shenice was all "Harry
this" and "Harry that", which Molly and I put up with
because Shen's never really had a crush on anyone before
and it's pretty cute.

I'm still trying my hardest to fight off the **GREEN-
EYED MONSTER** over their brilliant parts, but being in
the chorus is not helping. Yesterday we started setting
the scenes up onstage, working out what we had to do
and where we needed to be. I don't know if it is just me

but I find the whole stage right and stage left thing very confusing – stage right is only right if you are on the stage, otherwise it is left. And stage left is actually right if you are looking at the stage. Why not keep them the same as real life? Plus our dance captain, Charlotte, keeps telling us to "dance like no one is watching" but it's very hard to do that when actually there is someone watching and they keep telling you off when you get it wrong.

Anyway, if you'd asked me last week I would have told you that the last thing I wanted to do was stay in a rubbishy old caravan for a week but now I quite like the fact that no one will be shouting at me about scissor steps. Although at the rate this traffic is moving it will take us a week just to get there. Shenice's mum would probably have some kind of eco-theory for it but Dad says it's just the call of the beach.

"Stop moaning, Cassie," Mum said when I asked if we were nearly there yet. "Play some I-Spy with Liam."

Honestly, I think she has missed the last five years of our lives and thinks I am still six. Liam pulled his earbuds out. "What?"

"Mum wants us to play I-Spy," I told him.

He shrugged. "I spy, with my little eye, something beginning with L."

"Lorry," I said, gazing out of the window at the twisty country road. "Lamp post, legs, Lamborghini."

"Where?" he said, his head whipping around.

I smirked. "Oh sorry, it's a Mini. My mistake."

The game went on for another few minutes until I gave up. Liam looked straight at me and made an L sign on his forehead. "Loser."

There wasn't much I could say to that because he is absolutely right, I am a **LOSER**. Scowling, I slumped back in my seat. "Takes one to know one."

Still grinning, he put his headphones back in and the tinny sound of **WOLF BRETHREN**'s finest filled the car. I sighed and leaned forward. "Seriously, Mum, are we nearly there yet?"

Mum turned around to glare at me and I knew she was about to lose it. But then the car rounded a bend in the road and Dad gave a shout. "Yes! I can see the sea!" He pointed at the windscreen. "There!"

I squinted a bit in the sunshine and suddenly I could see it too – a shimmering mass of aquamarine underneath the paler blue of the sky. Even Liam looked excited and took his headphones out again.

"There's a sign for Happy Sands over there," he said,

pointing at the side of the road.

"Thank goodness for that," Mum said and even Rolo let out a small wuff of relief. We drove under a sign that read **WELCOME TO HAPPY SANDS**, with a huge palm tree on either side, and rolled slowly past caravan after caravan. And I started to realize that maybe I'd got the wrong idea about the kind of place we were going to stay in.

It wasn't an overgrown field after all and the caravans weren't the beaten-up types I was used to seeing blown up on old repeats of **TOP GEAR**. These were shiny and modern and nice. They weren't very mobile, either – some of them had decking attached to them and porches. In fact, a few of them looked like they might be even bigger than my nan's house.

The road we were driving on was smooth and lined with colourful flower beds, there was a gigantic glass dome in the distance that looked a lot like a waterpark and we passed several people in shorts carrying surfboards. Behind it all was the twinkling blue sea. It was the definition of awesome.

I exchanged a look with Liam. We'd both had our doubts when Mum and Dad had told us what their summer holiday plans were, but it seemed we couldn't have been more wrong. Liam wrapped his earbuds around his phone and tucked them carefully into his pocket.

"Last one in the pool is a moron," he said, grinning.

Okay, Happy Sands OFFICIALLY ROCKS.

Liam and I spent a couple of hours in the waterpark

and he only dunked me twice, and our
caravan is nothing like as titchy as
I thought it would be – there are
three bedrooms and two bathrooms
and a TV with at least some of the
good channels.

Dad says we can have surfing lessons down on the
beach, although I think it might be more fun to stay on
the sand and watch Liam fall off.

Anyway, the first night wasn't as disastrous as I was
expecting it to be. There was one minor incident in the
small hours of the night when Dad got up for a wee and
tripped over the twins' travel cot but he made more noise
than they did. You would think he had broken his toe the
way he went on. He insisted he couldn't take Rolo out for a
walk in the morning so I took him for a quick run while I
had a good nose around. The park is built around a village
bit in the middle, with a big entertainment complex called

THE HUB and some shops, restaurants and even a bowling alley. There's a path that leads down through some sand dunes to a gorgeous golden beach.

I snapped a photo and sent it to Molly and Shenice.

SUN + SAND + SEA = AWESOME. Wish you were here? XX

All in all, not too shabby. Maybe this holiday is just what I need to get over my shattered dreams.

I KNEW it was too good to be true. On the way back from Rolo's walk, I saw something that made my blood run cold. Outside THE HUB, where no one could possibly avoid seeing it, was a picture of my dad in all his Elvis finery. And underneath it said:

Happy Sands Holiday Villages
are proud to present,
for one week only,
THE POWER OF PRESLEY
Nightly in the Starlight Bar
9 pm

OMG, I think I might die. I really do. I thought he was JOKING when he talked about doing a deal by offering to perform. Seriously, what kind of father would do that to his kids? Even Victorian parents were not this cruel and they sent their children up chimneys. Liam is going to go nutso when he finds out. We are going to have to pretend we do not have a father. It is the only way.

Typically, Dad showed no signs of being sorry when I confronted him back at the caravan. He also refuses to cancel the booking, on the grounds that he is a professional and I of all people should understand that the show must go on.

Huh. The show mustn't go on. The show SHOULDN'T go on under any circumstances, not when it will cause severe emotional distress. It will be a disaster, anyway – no one will go. Surely the last thing people want when they are on holiday is to come and watch a middle-aged man dancing around in a wig and a onesie?

"It's a done deal," he said, shaking his head at me. "You don't have to come and see me but it would be nice if you could be a little more understanding."

I glanced over at Liam for help but he threw me a pitying look. "She doesn't get it, Dad. She's not a true performer."

"I am a performer, actually," I snapped back. "I've got a speaking part in the show."

"One line," Liam said, rolling his eyes. "Get that Oscar ready now."

OMG, he is so RUDE. He goes around acting like some kind of ROCK GOD but really no one outside of Windsor has heard of WOLF BRETHREN. And I don't know why my father can't be happy with his boring office job like everyone else's dad. I am starting to wish my talent was being able to turn invisible, then no one would know I exist, let alone that I am related to them.

Am I old enough to leave home yet?

The Little App of Calm

It is not what happens to you but how you react that matters – Epictetus

Sometimes, bad things happen that are outside of our control and it can be difficult to stay calm. When this happens, remember that the only person who can truly affect your mood is YOU. So take a step back and ask yourself, "Does this really matter? In a month's time, will anyone remember?"

Use the space below to record anything that may be troubling your mood today.

FAMILIES...
I CAN'T EVEN...
UGH.

CHAPTER NINE

Everyone has dreamed of running away at least once in their life – just them and a backpack on the open road.

When I tried, I only got as far as the beach and I forgot to take my backpack, although since it only has a dried-up glitter pen and my old half-filled UNICORN PALS notebook in it, that wasn't such a disaster.

Mum thought I was playing in the adventure playground – yet more evidence that she has forgotten

I am twelve in less than a month. Liam was supposed to be keeping an eye on me but he was playing the arcade games in the PlayZone and couldn't care less what I was doing.

It's strangely calming watching the waves crash onto the golden sand over and over again, impossible to stop, although they do remind me of the RELENTLESS SHAME-FEST that is my life. Miss Skelly told us that an actor must live in the moment while drawing from the past and I am trying to keep calm but it is hard when the past and the present are both made of utter HUMILIATION.

The beach next to the holiday camp isn't huge, but there were plenty of surfers out catching the waves. I know that Newquay is famous for surfing but it looks a bit dangerous to me. Still, it was good fun to watch, especially when someone caught a really big wave and looked like they were dancing on the top of it. It was almost enough to make me forget why I was hiding between the sand dunes in the first place.

"Alright, dweeb?" Liam said when he found me half an hour later. "I thought this was where you'd be."

I hate it when he does this, acts like he knows me when really he is an ALIEN from another planet sent to ruin my life. "What do you want?"

He sat down beside me. "I think you're being too harsh on Dad. I know he goes on and on about Elvis and I agree that outfit he wears is terrible but you have to give the audience what they expect." He glanced at me sideways. "You're wearing costumes for this show you're doing, right?"

The wardrobe mistress had measured me before I left so that they could get mine sorted out while I was away. All I knew was that it involved feathers. "Yeah."

"Well, imagine if you didn't wear it. Do you think the people watching would believe you were one of Fat Sam's dancers in 1920s New York?"

I stared at him, amazed for several reasons. I didn't realize he'd been paying attention when I'd been rattling on about the show. Normally he makes a big point of NOT listening. And he had a point about the costumes. "I suppose not."

"So it's the same for Dad. People expect a big black quiff and a satin jumpsuit – that's what Elvis wore. If Dad rocked up in his office clothes, no one would give him a second look."

I could see what he was getting at. "But why does he have to do it here? Everyone will know he's our dad. We're going to be laughing stocks."

I don't actually know what a laughing stock is but it

probably isn't good. Liam threw me a strange look. "Because staying somewhere like Happy Sands in the summer holidays isn't cheap and in case you haven't noticed, we don't have much cash to splash. I'm proud of Dad for getting booked for a solid week of performances. That doesn't happen unless you're good. And you don't get good unless you put the work in."

Call me a dumb salami, but it hadn't ever occurred to me that Dad might have had to work on his Elvis routine to perfect it, or even that he might be GOOD. All I'd thought about was how mortifying it was to have a parent who did what he did. I'd never realized he was just playing a part, basically the starring role in his own one-man show, but Liam was right – people don't pay unless you are good.

What was it Miss Skelly had said – something about a paying audience being hard to please? And I remembered how much my knees shook during my audition, and how

my heart felt like it was about to explode with terror.
If Dad felt like that every time he performed,
he didn't deserve my mockery.
He deserved a medal. ———⟶

"It hurt to get overlooked for the
part you wanted, right?" Liam asked.

I hugged my knees, remembering the sting of seeing
Imani's name on the wall instead of mine. "Yeah."

"Dad knows all about that — he's had plenty of failed
auditions and knock-backs in the early days but he didn't
let them grind him down and now he's finally becoming
successful. Forget for a minute that he's our dad and try
being supportive for once." He stared hard at me. "In
fact, try to be a bit more like your mate Molly."

I didn't need to ask what he meant — Molly was
WOLF BRETHREN's number-one fan and went way over

and above the call of duty to support them, although that was mostly because she fancied the disgusting three-day-old pants off Liam. But she'd done her best to help Shenice and me to up our audition game, too, even though she'd had her own song to learn. And then I thought about how expensive this holiday was, even though it might not be a lot for some families, and remembered that Mum and Dad had paid quite a lot of money to send me to EDDDA, on top of the bursary. And that was money Dad needed to earn all over again, by being Elvis when he should have been relaxing on holiday. Suddenly I felt brattier than a toddler in a tantrum.

Liam got up and brushed the sand off his shorts. "Stay away from the sea, okay? I don't want to get it in the neck because you've gone and drowned yourself."

He vanished into the dunes, leaving me with a TON of things to think about. As much as I hated to admit it, a lot of what he'd said made sense. Maybe it was time

I took a leaf out of Molly's book and started giving a little bit back.

I have decided that I must have been a mermaid in a former life. It is the only way I can explain my sudden yet deep-seated love of the sea. We spent all afternoon at the beach and Dad persuaded me to have my very first surfing lesson. I wasn't sure initially but I guess Miss Skelly's **PMA** mantra is really starting to sink in because I decided to give it a go.

Our teacher was this really cool girl called Alex, who I guessed was about seventeen or eighteen and looked like she might have been a mermaid in a previous life too, all wavy blonde tresses and sea-green eyes. I think Liam agrees because he could not stop looking at her and went red every time she spoke to him.

The first thing we learned was how to balance, face down, on our boards. Wait – actually, the first thing we learned was how to put on a wetsuit because even in the summer, the sea is cold. Wearing a wetsuit basically involves climbing into a second skin – a chilly, super-tight second skin that does not want to be climbed into and fights you at every stage. But eventually, we battled them into submission. Then Alex taught us how to paddle across the waves close to the shore and how to pick out the good waves from the bad.

"You need to feel each wave," she said, her eyes scanning the sea. "Learn the way they rise and fall and make them your friend."

I half expected Liam to snort with laughter but he was nodding like it was the wisest thing he'd ever heard.

That was when I knew he was trying to impress her. Still, I couldn't really blame him — she was super cool. If I was a wave I'd be her friend.

Next, she showed us how to crouch on the board. Liam tried to show off and wiped out almost right away. He surfaced, coughing and spluttering. Alex waded over to check on him. Learning from his mistake, I visualized myself standing on the board and slowly pushed myself up.

"Epic work, Cassie," Alex said, looking pleased. "You've got really good posture too."

Mum actually cheered in her deckchair. Liam glared at me, as though I was doing it on purpose to make him look bad. "You gotta either go hard or go home, that's what I say. YOLO, right?"

Honestly, sometimes I think he really is an alien.

"What are you talking about?" I said, dredging up as much scorn as I could manage. "What even is YOLO?"

He fired a pitying look my way. "It stands for You Only Live Once. Don't you know anything?"

It sounded like typical Liam rubbish. He is such a MORON and I'm sure he makes most of this stuff up — of course we only live once, we are not cats.

"I don't need YOLO," I told him, paddling my board into the waves once more. "I've got a PMA."

He mumbled something back but I was too busy watching the waves to listen. Spotting a good one, I pushed myself upright, rode my board into the shallows and jumped neatly off.

"Awesome, Cassie!" Alex shouted, giving me a round

of applause that Liam grudgingly joined in with. "You've got it!"

I felt a warm glow of pride but obviously I couldn't take all the credit. Who knew Miss Skelly's PMA would work for surfing as well as acting? And I couldn't wait to tell Molly her visualization trick had worked.

"Did I tell you I'm in a band?" Liam said to Alex as we walked back to the surf school building with our boards. "We're called WOLF BRETHREN because we answer the call of the wild."

I had to bite my lip really hard not to giggle. That kind of chat-up line might work on Molly or one of his other fans but Alex was used to hanging with loads of cool surfer types. She wasn't going to be interested in Liam, no matter what he said the band did.

"That's great," she said, smiling. "What do you play?"

I could practically see Liam's chest swell. "Guitar. But I'm also the lead singer. We rock pretty hard, right, Cass?"

I thought carefully before I answered. On one hand, it was a solid-gold opportunity to get Liam back for all the insults and sneers he'd sent my way in the last few weeks. But on the other, he'd been almost helpful earlier when we'd talked about Dad, and WOLF BRETHREN were almost legends at St Jude's. So I nodded. "Yeah. They rock."

It turned out Alex played the guitar too so they swapped stories all the way back to the surf school.

"Same time tomorrow?" Alex said, once we were out of our wetsuits.

"You'd better believe it," Liam said, raising one eyebrow and smiling. "Watch out, surf-rats. The sea wolf is on the prowl."

OMG, that line is cheesier than Rolo's breath. Liam is such a dumb salami!

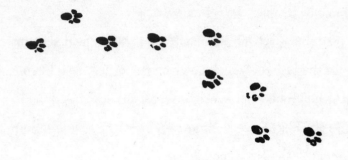

CHAPTER TEN

The weirdest thing happened on Friday morning. I was walking past the waterpark with Rolo, trying to stop him from eating a rose bush, when I heard Dad's name mentioned. There was a man talking into a mobile phone, looking at the poster. My first instinct was to run but something made me sidle closer. I really hoped Rolo would understand we were in STEALTH MODE or my cover was going to be blown sky-high.

"Yeah, The Power of Presley," the man said into the

handset. "We saw it last night and it's a cracking show – this guy practically is The King! Just get here for nine o'clock tonight. It's almost sold out already."

He wandered away, leaving me staring after him in amazement. Almost sold out? Had I heard that right? Wow. Maybe it was time to find out what The Power of Presley was all about.

"I think it's a great idea," Mum said, when I got back to the caravan and asked her about watching Dad perform. Dad and Liam had taken the twins to the soft play area and it was just me and her. "You might be pleasantly surprised. I know I was, all those years ago."

I don't know if you've ever tried to imagine how your parents got together but it's totally weird. For one thing, they were obviously never young and have always looked like they do now. It's also a bit icky to imagine them being all LOVEY-DOVEY with each other. If Mum ever thought Dad looked **HOT** in his Elvis get-up then her love goggles must have been seriously strong. She hardly ever talks about how they met, something I'm usually glad about because, let's face it, it's got **"CRINGESOME TO THE MAX"** written all over it.

"Of course, he was a lot slimmer in those days," she said, a wistful look in her eyes. "And I had a thing about singers. He looked like Robbie from **TAKE THAT**, or what Robbie would have looked like if he'd ever dressed up as Elvis, and he picked me out of the audience to sing **LOVE ME TENDER**. That was it – I was hooked."

The whole conversation should have been setting off every awkwardness klaxon known to mankind but somehow it wasn't. Maybe it was because I'd never heard this story before, or maybe because it was making me see yet another side of my dad I hadn't known was there.

"When was the last time you went to see him perform?" I asked.

She laughed and rubbed her forehead in a tired way. "Oh, not since before the twins were born. Hang on, maybe not since before you were born. I used to take Liam with me sometimes but it got too difficult once there were two of you."

I thought back to what Liam had said the day before. I cringed every time I saw Dad in his Elvis outfit so he must realize how embarrassing I found it. But how would I feel if the tables were turned and Dad refused to come and see me deliver my single line in the EDDDA show?

"So you think I should be more supportive too," I said.

She smiled. "I think Dad would love it if you went to see him perform. Why don't you ask Liam, see if he wants to go too?"

"Because then I would have to admit I know him and be seen with him in public," I said, in the same tone of voice I used on the twins.

Mum threw me a weary look. "Just go and catch the performance, Cassie. Who knows, you might actually learn something."

And that's when she pushed it too far. I mean SERIOUSLY, what kind of world would it be if we all went around LEARNING STUFF from our parents?

I didn't know what to expect when I took my seat in the Starlight Bar to watch Dad's show. I mean OBVIOUSLY I had some idea – there'd be a lot of Elvis for a start and probably some ridiculously embarrassing hip thrusts but I didn't know whether I was about to enjoy myself or DIE trying. I was determined to stay positive, though — my PMA was starting to kick in and I wasn't about to give it up.

The bar was packed — almost every table was full. I'd expected it to be mostly old people but there were quite a few younger guests too. Strictly speaking, under-fourteens weren't allowed in the bar unaccompanied after nine o'clock but they bent the rules for me since technically, I'd be in the same room as Dad, just not right next to him. I couldn't really escape from sitting with Liam, though. He'd clearly got the MEMO about pretending not to know each other because he completely ignored me and that suited me fine.

I thought I spotted Alex, working behind the bar, and judging from the way Liam kept looking around, he'd seen her too. But then the lights dimmed and a single spotlight lit the stage. "Ladies and Gentlemen, Happy Sands Holiday Village Newquay is proud to welcome to the stage, THE POWER OF PRESLEY!"

Music began to pound out of the speakers and I recognized the start of A LITTLE LESS CONVERSATION, one of Dad's favourite songs. He bounded onto the stage and grabbed the microphone, dropping Liam and me a huge wink before he started to sing.

I never thought I'd say this but Dad is an awesome Elvis! He was so good that I almost forgot he was my dad and actually started to believe he was The King. What was even cooler is that the audience clearly thought he was amazing too — they whooped

and clapped and cheered so much that he had to do two
encores. One woman threw a pair of pants at the stage
— I'm SO glad Rolo was safely back at the caravan with
Mum or there might have been a KNICKER NICKING
DISASTER.

Anyway, Dad totally owned the stage and it's pretty
obvious where Liam gets his love of performing from.
I suppose that's where mine comes from too, although I'm
definitely not feeling the love as much as I was before
I missed out on Lena. I'm really starting to get what Molly
meant when she said fame costs — a true performer dusts
themselves off after each setback and tries again, no
matter how rubbish they feel. Dad hadn't let a failed
audition hold him back — he'd just worked even harder.
Maybe I COULD learn something from him after all.

"Well?" Dad asked, when he met us outside the stage
door, minus his Elvis outfit and looking normal again.
"What did you think — any good?"

"Good?" I squeaked. "You were brilliant!"

Liam held out a fist. "Yeah, nice one."

As we started to walk back to the caravan, Dad and I chatted about the show but Liam kept looking over his shoulder. "Listen, I think I might just go back and – um – check whether I left my phone behind."

Sometimes his stupidity amazes even me. "The one that's in your hand, you mean?" I said, staring at him in disbelief. "That phone?"

His face flamed red. Ignoring me, he turned and hurried back towards The Hub.

"Let him go," Dad said, grinning. "There'll be a girl involved, I expect."

Poor Alex, I thought. But I didn't mind that Liam was

about to make a GIGANTIC fool of himself because it gave me the chance to say something that had been on my mind from the moment Dad had started his performance. Taking a deep breath, I blurted out my apology.

"I'm sorry I shouted at you yesterday for working here. And I'm sorry I said that your quiff looked like you bought it in the Pound Shop, and that your suit is two sizes too small. I don't really cry myself to sleep wishing you were like Molly's dad and...and...well, if you tell anyone this I will deny everything but sometimes I like it when you sing Elvis around the house."

Dad chuckled. "It's okay, I understand," he said, patting me on the arm. "Believe it or not, I was your age once and my parents were just as embarrassing."

It is practically impossible to imagine your parents as children, even when there is photographic evidence that they have not always been ancient. And it is even more impossible to imagine your grandparents when they were young.

"Really?" I said, wondering what terrible crimes of fashion and/or parenting my father had suffered. "Why?"

He shrugged. "They were ballroom dancers. They used to enter these contests and dragged me along to watch, when all my friends were listening to the pop charts. It took me a long time to realize that they were actually really good dancers."

I tried to picture my grandparents doing STRICTLY COME DANCING and failed. "Oh."

"Eventually I realized I hated the music they played on the radio," Dad went on. "The stuff I loved best was on the crackly old records my dad used to play on a Sunday afternoon. They made me want to be a singer when I grew up."

"So how come you only sing Elvis?" I asked, because I couldn't help thinking it would have been pretty cool if Dad had become a famous pop star instead. We'd have our own helicopter and a huge house and I'd have more knickers than Rolo could get through in a lifetime.

"Someone told me I'd make a really good Elvis. Of course, plenty of people said I'd be a terrible Elvis, too. But I practised and watched a lot of Elvis performances and eventually, I got into his head and the bookings started to roll in." He smiled. "I suppose you could say it's my THING."

I smiled back. "Being Elvis is TOTALLY your thing."

He twisted his lip in his weird Power of Presley way and did an over-exaggerated hip thrust. "Uh huh huh."

Okay, so maybe he can still be a bit embarrassing. But you know what? I think I can live with that.

I've slipped into a routine in the four days we've been here. In the morning, I take Rolo for a stroll along the beach and help Mum with the twins. Dad is basking in the glow of his new-found fame and even has people coming to ask him for autographs — it is totally insane.

In the afternoon, I hang around the waterpark pretending not to know Liam, or I join in with one of the activities. Shenice is going to be so proud of me when I show her the certificate I got from Crusty and the Crab Crew for helping them to clear up abandoned cans and plastic bottles. It's even signed by Crusty himself, although how he could even hold the pen with those pincers is a ↗ mystery. Then, at four o'clock every day, we go surfing with Alex.

Surfing is the best, I messaged Molly and Shenice on Saturday, after our third lesson. *Believe it or not, I know how to paddle out, pop up onto the board and ride a proper wave now! I can change direction too. It's definitely not Liam's thing – he can hardly stand up and keeps bailing before he wipes out. Dad says he's eaten more sand than a camel this week. Oh, and he's scared of jellyfish! He claims he's not but he goes all funny when he sees one on the beach.*

Our teacher says I'm a natural surfer, which I'm totally stoked about. She says I should keep learning but I don't see how I can unless there is a secret beach in Windsor I don't know about. So I'm just living in the moment and enjoying it while I can.

How are rehearsals going?

C xx

Total nightmare, Molly messaged me. *No one knows the dances, Fat Sam's hoodlums have got some kind of feud going on and I think Miss Skelly hates me. Shenice is mooning around after Harry like he's some kind of rock star. He might be a good actor but he's definitely no Liam. M xx*

Hi Cass. OMG, you won't believe how badly things are going! Shenice texted. *Harry and me are fine but Molly spends all her time moaning on about how much she misses Liam. She's obsessed with the idea that he's going to have a holiday fling – honestly, what does she see in him? Harry is a big Wolf Brethren fan, btw.*

Hurry up and come home – I miss you! Harry says HI! S xx

I genuinely have no idea what Molly sees when she looks at Liam and I'm pretty sure Alex doesn't see it either.

She is way too cool to notice him — she's quite possibly the coolest person in the entire universe. On Sunday morning, I saw her catching some waves when I took Rolo for his walk and she is totally amazing. I want to be her when I grow up.

I made Rolo sit down while I watched her work the water. I really got what she meant about being one with the wave — she looked like she'd been carved out of glass as she rode across the surface of the sea and then she did this epic jump. Rolo seemed impressed too, because he sat really still until she waded to the shore.

Most people think all dogs love water: Rolo is not one of those dogs. In fact, he has an extreme aversion to water — as we discovered the first time we put him in the bath and almost flooded the kitchen underneath. He hates it, from the smallest speck of rain to the undignified soaking with the hosepipe that has replaced the indoor bath. All of which made it even more ASTONISHING that

he apparently decided today was the day he was going
to feel the fear and do it anyway. Jumping up, he lurched
forwards, tugging the lead out of my relaxed fingers.
It was the last thing I was expecting him to do.

"Rolo!" I bellowed as he took off across the sand. "Get
back here, you bad dog!"

He bounded away, tail held high, aiming for the water
as though his fur was on fire. I raced after him, hoping he
would lose interest in whatever had caught his eye. No
such luck – his beady eyes were fixed on Alex as she
waded to shore and he tore across the sand like she was
made of cheese. "Rolo, NO!"

Alex looked up just as Rolo reached the breakers. And
all of a sudden it dawned on his minuscule doggy brain
that the bubbling white stuff was his arch-nemesis,
WATER. But he was too close to stop. Instead, he made
a desperate leap for her surfboard, landing on it with a

scrabbling of claws
and a desperate
yelp. I expected
him to slide
right off the
other side but
somehow he clung on
and managed to stay upright.

"Sorry," I puffed as I arrived at the water's edge.
"My dog...bit mad...Rolo...get off. OFF!"

"Don't worry," she said, putting one hand on his back
to help him balance. "He just wants to catch some radical
rip curls, don't you, boy?"

"Can dogs do that?" I asked, my eyes widening
in amazement. Rolo certainly seemed to be enjoying
himself – his tongue was lolling out of his mouth in a
happy-dog grin.

"Of course," she said. "In California, they have surfing competitions especially for dogs. Maybe Rolo is a future champion surfdog!"

Ha, she's clearly never seen the lengths he goes to avoid an appointment with the hosepipe. But he seemed pretty comfortable on the board and the idea of seeing him surf some waves was tempting – imagine if it turned out he was better than Liam? "Can we try?"

Alex glanced out to sea at the waves. "It looks pretty clean but I don't have a life jacket for him so we'll have to stay near the shore." She threw me a sunny smile. "But we can still teach him a trick or two."

I didn't think it was possible for Alex to get any cooler but she seriously turned into a sea goddess that morning. By the time she'd finished with Rolo, he'd gone from water-phobic to water baby. Every time he slid off into the sea, she helped him back on and soon he was riding the waves and cruising to the shore. I was so proud of him I thought I might burst.

"The trick is to fake it until you make it, Rolo," she said. "Never let anyone see you're clucked. That's what gets me through the really big waves."

CLUCKED? Surely chickens didn't surf too? And then I realized it was surfer slang for scared.

I couldn't imagine Alex being afraid of anything. She seemed like one of those super-confident people who could do anything. "Really?"

"Really," she said. "The thing no one ever tells you is that everyone feels the same way ninety-nine per cent of the time, worried and unsure. We've all got that little voice telling us we can't do it. The secret is to do whatever it is anyway."

"So I suppose you might say you've got a positive mental attitude," I said slowly. "The principal at my drama academy calls it a PEE EM AIEE."

Alex snapped her fingers. "That's exactly what it is. You've got a PMA too, haven't you, Rolo? Every time you fall off, you get straight back on and try again."

Rolo gave a gigantic woof. Then he cocked his head to one side and leaped off the board, racing over the sand towards a figure in the distance. Groaning, I started to chase him again, before realizing the figure was Dad.

"We thought you'd fallen in, Cass," he called cheerfully once he was near enough. "But it looks like the victim was Rolo."

Alex was staring at Dad like he'd just fallen from PLANET CELEBRITY. "Great show last night," she said in a star-struck voice, before glancing at me. "You're so lucky to have such a rad dad."

Dad laughed. "Rad dad...I might get that put on a T-shirt."

"Alex has been teaching Rolo to surf," I told him. "She says he's a natural."

He turned an astonished look on Rolo. "Really?"

"I know!" I said, shrugging like I couldn't believe it either. "But it's true. Surfing seems to be his THING. And at least when he's surfing, he's not eating my pants."

"True," Dad said, pulling a face. "It's a shame we live so far from the beach, eh, Rolo?"

It was a real shame, I decided, as we said goodbye to Alex and walked back to the caravan. Because between

Rolo's surfing and Dad's Elvis, the Bond family were going down a storm in Cornwall. At the risk of sounding even cheesier than Liam, we were licensed to THRILL.

Cassie's Surfing Fact-o-rama

* Surfing has been around for centuries – Captain James Cook saw it in Hawaii in 1778 and described it as "the most supreme pleasure".

* You can study Surf Science at university – so cool!

* The Guinness World Record for the most people EVER to stand on a surfboard is 47 – must have been a big board!

* Surfers only spend eight per cent of their time actually surfing. The rest of the time is spent paddling and waiting for waves. Or, if you are Liam, WIPING OUT.

* The fear of waves is called cymophobia.

* MEN IN GREY SUITS
is surfing slang
for sharks.

* The chances of being attacked by a shark while
surfing is around one in 11 million and it's even
less in Cornwall. PHEW!

CHAPTER ELEVEN

Word has started to get around about Rolo the Radical Surfdog. As we've got nearer to the end of our holiday, he's become almost as famous as Dad. We bought him a doggy life jacket from one of the surf shops in Newquay and Alex didn't mind him joining in with our surf lessons, mostly because it meant more people were booking lessons, although not for their dogs. The local paper came and snapped some photos, which they put up online with the headline: YOLO ROLO! Huh, maybe that isn't something Liam made up after all.

Molly and Shenice have been keeping me in the EDDDA loop.

Hi Cass, Molly wrote. Same old same old here – you'll be pleased to know Imani is a terrible Lena – she can hardly carry a tune and I think the musical director is going to have a nervous breakdown if she sings flat one more time. Our costumes are hideous and S is STILL mooning around after H. I think she wishes she'd gone for Blousey because she keeps going on about the number of scenes I have with him. She's nervous about the KISSING scene – they haven't practised it yet!

Hope you are still having fun, catching the waves. How's Liam? Say hi for me. Loved that photo of Rolo surfing – TOTALLY RAD! M xx

Ugh, things have hit rock bottom here, Shenice texted. My Tallulah dress doesn't fit! None of the *costumes do – Molly's Blousey coat looks like a family of six could camp under it. The boy who was playing Knuckles has quit but it's okay, Miss Skelly asked someone else to step up. Anyway, everyone is doing their best but Harry says there's no way we're going to be performance-ready by show night. Save yourself and stay there! S xx*

PS Was that really Rolo surfing? He's looks better than Liam!

If you'd asked me at the start of the holiday if I wanted to stay longer, I would definitely have said yes. But Dad has shown me you have to go all in as a performer to get anything back. Together with my PMA, I can't actually WAIT to get back to BUGSY MALONE. I'm still a bit disappointed about missing out on Lena (especially if Imani is as bad as Molly says) but I'm going to give the show 110 per cent.

I just wish Mum could see Dad's show while we're here. But she won't let Liam and me babysit the twins on our own and tonight is his last performance. I wonder if Auntie Jane can hitch a lift on a helicopter or something?

I can't believe it's our last surf lesson with Alex — the holiday has gone so fast. How am I going to indulge my mermaid tendencies when I live a zillion miles away from the beach? Wallowing in the bath just won't be the same. Liam is even more devastated — I think he may actually be in LOVE with Alex and has been desperately trying to find a way to spend more time with her, with the emphasis on DESPERATE. It would be funny if it wasn't so toe-curling.

Mum brought the twins down to the beach for our final lesson. She cheered as I zoomed along the top of the waves and cutback neatly. Even Liam managed to stay on long enough for Mum to snap some photos. Afterwards, the twins paddled at the water's edge. Alex smiled as they gurgled in delight. "They're so cute. My sister has a little girl and she's exactly the same – a real water baby."

Ethel wobbled and splashed down onto her bottom. For a moment, she looked like she might cry, then she flapped her hands in the foaming waves and laughed. Alex crouched down next to her and patted the water too, sending more foam bubbling over Ethel's legs. Joshua crawled over to see what the fun was about and all three of them sat among the breakers, laughing and splashing.

"You're very good with them," Mum said, smiling.

Alex looked up, squinting in the sun. "Yeah, I babysit for my sister a lot. I love babies."

And then it hit me – LIGHT BULB! Why hadn't I thought of it before?

"Alex," I said, trying to keep the excitement out of my voice. "What are you doing tonight?"

It's pretty obvious who got all the theatrical talent in our family and it wasn't Liam. But that doesn't stop him from trying.

"I don't think I'll have any tea," he said once we'd gone back to the caravan and he'd finished in the shower. "I've got a monster headache."

He raised one hand to touch his forehead and pulled the same expression the twins do when they're filling their nappies. I almost burst out laughing – he couldn't have been any more obvious if he'd had a flashing neon sign over his head saying "I AM FAKING".

I'm pretty sure Mum saw right through it as well but she just nodded. "Okay. Why don't you have a little lie-down and see if that helps? You wouldn't want to miss your dad's last show."

Ha, unless I was completely wrong, that was EXACTLY what Liam wanted. I waited until he'd taken himself off to his room, then sneaked around the back and peered through his window. Sure enough, he was propped up on the bed with his headphones in and the music blasting out was loud enough for me to recognize the lyrics to HOWLING AT THE MOON. I knew it! He was throwing a sickie so he could spend the evening babysitting the twins with Alex. Shaking my head, I backed away and went to get ready. Only on PLANET LIAM could anyone be so deluded.

He reappeared when Alex knocked at the door. Mum was still getting ready so I got up to answer and suddenly Liam's door flew back and he practically knocked me out

of the way to get there first. "Feeling better, are we?"
I said in my sarkiest voice.

Ignoring me, he yanked back the door. "Hi, Alex.
You look nice."

Ugh, pass the sick bucket, **PLEASE**. Alex smiled and
thanked him, even though she didn't look any different to
normal, except for not wearing a wetsuit. "Hey, Alex. The
twins are through here," I called from the living room.

Mum popped her head out of the bedroom. "Hi, Alex,
thanks for coming. Kids, will you be ready in five minutes?"

I nodded but Liam instantly put on his poorly face
again. "Urgh, Mum, my head is killing me. Maybe I'd better
sit tonight out."

I snorted loudly. "Get over it, Liam. Alex doesn't want
to babysit you too."

If looks could kill, I'd be dead and buried. I smiled sweetly back. Now I could get my revenge for all the times he'd dunked me in the waterpark over the last week. And boy was it going to feel good.

Mum came over and felt his forehead. "You don't have a temperature. Have you drunk enough water today?"

Liam nodded meekly. "I've tried to."

She studied him for a long moment, then sighed. "Okay. You can stay here, as long as Alex doesn't mind?"

Alex looked up from the floor, where she was playing with Joshua and Ethel. "No, that's fine. You can tell me all about the WOLVES, Liam."

His face lit up. Then he seemed to remember he was supposed to be ill and he gave a little cough.

"Maybe. If I feel well enough."

Mum turned away and headed back to her room. As she went, her eye caught mine and I swear she dropped me the faintest of sly winks. Liam was fooling no one.

She came back out a few minutes later, wearing a beautiful sea-green dress. She looked lovely.

"We'll be back just after ten o'clock," she told Alex and handed her a piece of paper. "This is my mobile number in case you need anything but obviously Liam knows how to get hold of me."

"Thanks," Alex said, taking the number. "I'm sure I won't need to trouble you."

"They should go off to sleep as soon as they've had their milk. And Liam, mind you don't pester Alex," Mum said. "She's here to look after the babies, not you."

"MUM!" Liam groaned, turning red. "Just go already."

She bent to kiss each of the twins. "I'll see you soon."
Straightening up, she looked anxiously at Alex. "Call if you
need me."

"We'll be fine, Mrs Bond," Alex reassured her. "Have
a great time."

I checked my phone – it was almost eight-thirty.
"We need to go, Mum."

With one final worried glance, she headed for the door.
"Bye, Liam. Be good."

I couldn't believe how packed the bar was. All the tables
were full and people were standing in every available
space. For a moment I worried we wouldn't get in, but
then one of the staff members recognized us and led us to

a reserved table at the front.
No sooner had we settled into
our seats than the lights dipped.
"Ladies and gentlemen, Happy
Sands Holiday Village Newquay
is proud to present, for his final
performance, THE POWER OF
PRESLEY!"

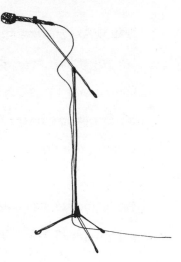

I know this is hard to believe but Dad was even better
than he was the last time I saw him. I don't know whether
he was making an extra-special effort because Mum was
there, or whether it was the people who got up and danced,
but the atmosphere was amazing. And I'm pretty sure even
the barman was snivelling when Dad dedicated I OVE ME
TENDER to "his beautiful wife". It was a night to
remember for so many reasons, and I was super proud
of them both. And this time, I remembered to snap a photo
to send to Molly and Shenice.

NO WAY! Shenice replied instantly. That can't be your dad. He looks amazing! S xx

PS Really looking forward to seeing you! M is driving me nutso...

Wow, Molly messaged me back. You were totally right – he IS The King. M xx

PS We NEED to talk about Shen. I am pretty sure she thinks I am trying to steal Harry!

It sounds like I am heading home at exactly the right time – I will be like a United Nations Peacekeeping envoy, sent to diffuse tensions before a full-scale war can erupt. Hmmm...I wonder if I can make a helmet out of seashells before we go tomorrow?

"Everything okay?" Mum asked Alex when we all got back to the caravan.

She nodded. "No problems at all. The twins went to sleep without a problem and Liam seems to be feeling better too."

Ha, he didn't look better – in fact, he looked as though he was about to burst into tears. Wow, he really did have it bad. I'd better keep my mouth zipped about that when I get home or the toys would REALLY come out of Molly's pram.

Alex came over to give me a hug. "Well done, Cassie, you and Rolo are both surfing superstars. I hope you're going to keep it up?"

I grinned. "Are you kidding? Just try and stop me!"

She waved at Liam. "Good luck with the band. They sound really cool."

He mumbled something I didn't catch, staring at his

feet as though the bottom had dropped out of his world. I almost felt sorry for him. Almost.

Mum held out some money. "Thanks so much, Alex. We had a great time."

"You're welcome," Alex said and she waved at us all one final time. "See you around!"

The moment the caravan door closed, Liam started shuffling towards his room. "Night," he muttered in a small voice.

Dad waited until he was almost through the door before he spoke. "Cheer up, Liam. They've booked me again for next year!"

Liam paused and his shoulders became ever so slightly less droopy. "Oh," he said, sounding a bit more cheerful. "Night!"

I went to bed then too. I don't know if it was all the fresh air or the anticipation of seeing Molly and Shenice again but I fell asleep the moment my head hit the pillow. Cornwall is great but I'm ready to go home. And I can't wait to get back to the academy, especially now that my PMA has had a serious boost. Watch out, EDDDA – Cassie's coming atcha!

To: <u>BondGirl007</u>

From: <u>NathanC</u>

Hi Cassie,

How are you? I think you must be in sunny Cornwall right now – how's the surf looking?

Anyway, the reason I'm writing is because we're coming home early! Dad's business plans have changed and we don't need to stay here for quite so long, so his work is getting us a flight home at the end of this week. I can't wait to see you and catch up with what everyone has been doing. Maybe we can get a sundae at the Shake Shack, if you're not too busy with rehearsing...

See you soon!

Nathan

CHAPTER TWELVE

Rolo gave me the most disappointed look ever on Thursday morning, when I packed my bag and headed out to Molly's car. He laid his head on his paws and huffed.

"Sorry, boy, it's back to normal for you," I said, ruffling his ears. "Maybe I'll get the paddling pool out later and we can pretend we're at the beach."

Molly and Shenice had come round the evening before to get the lowdown on my holiday, and I'd given them the shell necklaces I'd bought from one of the souvenir shops in Newquay. On the surface, everything seemed fine — they oohed and ahhed over my descriptions of surfing and loved the video of Rolo surfing I'd taken on my phone — but there was definitely an undercurrent of tension, exactly the kind of thing Alex had taught me to watch out for in the water.

Once we really got talking, the situation at the academy didn't sound like it had improved much.

"Don't ask about the dancing," Shenice said, groaning. "You know that TV presenter on Strictly who couldn't remember their left from their right? Times that by about ten."

"But you guys are okay?" I asked. "You're enjoying yourselves?"

"Shenice certainly is," Molly said, winking.

"Shut up," Shenice said, going red. "Harry and me are just friends."

"Friends who kiss," Molly said.

Shenice blushed even more. "Well, yeah. Although Bugsy does choose Blousey over Tallulah in the end."

Remembering Molly's message, I changed the subject. "But it's all coming together, right? I mean, it's only nine days until the show. It'll be alright on the night?"

Molly and Shenice exchanged doubtful looks. "Maybe," Shenice said.

"It's not all bad news, though," Molly said, with a sudden smile. "We've got a big surprise for you."

"What?" I demanded but they wouldn't tell me.

"Wait and see," was all they would say.

The general air of chaos on stage wasn't helped by me — it took a while to remember where I was meant to be and I bumped into more than one person as I fumbled my way around the stage. But every time I thought I might lose my cool, I pictured myself back on the beach in Cornwall, paddling over the turquoise waves on my board, and my irritation melted away. Some of the dances had changed, so I had an extra lunchtime lesson with the dance captain, Charlotte, and got to the canteen very late. Molly and Shenice were acting weird. They kept looking at each other and smiling in a "We know something you don't know" way.

"Okay, what's going on?" I demanded after a few minutes. "What's with the Smuggly Smuggerson routine?"

"She hasn't noticed," Shenice said in a stage whisper.

"I know," Molly whispered back. "I can't believe it. Should've gone to Specsavers or what?"

I stared at them in growing frustration. What? **WHAT?** And then I caught a glimpse of familiar blond hair across the room and leaned sharply sideways to look around them. There, on the other side of the canteen, was Nathan.

I gasped. "What? How is that possible?"

"He came home early," Molly explained. "His dad's—"

"I know that," I interrupted. "What's he doing here?"

Molly bristled a bit. "I was just about to tell you, Miss Stroppy Pants. He's enrolled on the stage-management course."

I gasped. "He said he'd enrolled but wasn't going to make it because of his holiday!"

"Which was cut short," Molly said. "So here he is."

Shenice smirked. "See, told you we had a surprise for you."

There's a moment in the film GREASE, where Danny and Sandy discover they're at the same high school after their summer fling. And you can almost see the love hearts EXPLODING ⟶ over their heads. That was how I felt when Nathan glanced around the room and his eyes came to rest on me. I waved. Grinning, he waved back and started weaving through the tables towards me.

"Hey," he said. "How was Cornwall?"

"Cool," I replied, beaming. "How was Australia?"

"Also cool," he said. "But it's good to be home."

"Yeah," I said. The bell rang, meaning it was time to head back into our rehearsals. "Maybe I'll see you around?"

"I hope so," he said, smiling. "There's a SUGAR RUSH MOUNTAIN →
at the Shake Shack with our name on it and I can't wait to hear about the waves you aced."

I stood up and tried to play it cool. "Great. So I'll see you later, then."

He nodded. "See you later."

Thankfully, Molly and Shenice waited until he was well out of earshot to start squealing.

"Oh shush," I told them.

But the truth was I could have skipped onto the stage after that. I didn't, obviously, but I could have. Cornwall had been brilliant but it didn't have my BFFs and it didn't have Nathan. Dorothy from THE WIZARD OF OZ had a point. There really is no place like home.

Over the next few days I caught up with everything I'd missed and was starting to think maybe – just maybe – Miss Skelly wasn't going to make me hang up my acting boots. It was fun watching Molly and Shenice do their scenes – Molly really sparkled and Shenice was amazing too. And it didn't matter how much Shenice protested that she liked Harry as a friend, I saw how she looked at him onstage and no matter how good at acting she'd become, she wasn't **THAT** good. She had a bona fide, ginormous crush on Harry. And when I saw him chasing around after Molly as Blousey onstage, it gave me a bad feeling. Shenice was watching them too, with a funny, narrow-eyed expression. The last thing any of us needed was for her to get the wrong idea about Molly.

In the breaks between scenes and at lunchtime, I helped them both with their lines. We took it in turns to host a Bugsy rehearsal at our houses, too – Friday night had been at my house, Saturday was at Shenice's and Sunday was Molly's turn. We went through every song and every line of dialogue over and over. Liam complained that he could hear us in the garage over his **WOLF BRETHREN** rehearsal, which only made us sing louder. We were practically eating, breathing and sleeping **BUGSY MALONE** and by the following Tuesday, I knew both of their parts backwards.

And then, halfway through Wednesday morning,

disaster struck. We'd just come offstage after the Fat
Sam's Grand Slam number and the darkened wings were
full of chorus members and principals. Some of the
hoodlums were messing about, pushing and shoving each
other and pretending they had machine guns.

"Oh yeah?" shouted the boy playing Yonkers Charlie.
"Eat metal, ya monkeys!"

Fat Sam's gang staggered as though they'd been shot.
One of them lurched backwards into Shenice. She let out a
yelp and tumbled over a chair that one of the stagehands
was carrying. There was a sickening crack and a thud,
followed by a painful-sounding gasp. And then Shenice
started to cry – loud, racking sobs – and my heart fell
into my feet. Because if she was making that much noise,
it was bad – really bad.

Fighting my way through the hoodlums, I hovered by
her side. "What is it, Shen? Where does it hurt?"

"My leg," she moaned in between sobs. "It really hurts."

Nick appeared and Molly was right behind him. "Everyone clear out," he commanded. "Back to the dance studio. We'll take a fifteen-minute break."

Shenice clutched at my hand. "Don't leave me."

Nick crouched down. "It's okay, Cassie and Molly can stay. I'm a first-aider, Shenice. Where does it hurt?"

"Her leg," I said, as Shen started to wail even louder. "One of the boys knocked her over and there was this sort of crack and—"

"I get the idea," Nick said in a grim voice. He knelt down next to Shenice and checked her leg. Then he glanced over his shoulder at Charlotte, the dance captain. "Let Miss Skelly know we're going to need an ambulance.

And get Shenice's
mum on the
phone."

It was so hard seeing Shen in pain without being able
to do anything to help. Molly and I tried to make her
laugh, but even our best jokes seemed a bit rubbish and it
was a relief when the paramedics arrived. We moved out
of the way while they checked her over and transferred
her onto a stretcher.

"Suspected broken leg," one of them told Miss Skelly.
"We'll know for sure after an X-ray."

Molly and I stared at each other. Molly looked pale
and shocked. We've had some scrapes and bumps over the
years but none of us has ever broken any bones. Shenice's
mum arrived then, rushing onto the stage behind
Charlotte just as the paramedics lifted the stretcher.
They carried Shenice through the wings.

"See you soon, Shen!" I called, biting my lip with worry.

"Take it easy," Molly shouted.

Miss Skelly and Nick followed, leaving Molly and me alone on the stage.

"This is bad," Molly said slowly. "If that leg is broken then she won't be able to perform on Friday."

I shook my head sadly. "Never mind her leg, her heart's going to be broken – there's no way she can play Tallulah on crutches, which means she can't kiss Harry either. What are we going to do?"

Molly sighed. "You know what they say, the show must go on. But I don't know who's going to be able to take over the role. It's only two days until the show."

The backstage door swung open and Nick strode back

onto the stage. "She's gone to A&E. They'll look after her there."

Molly gazed at him, her eyes wide and troubled. "Is she going to be okay?"

He smiled in sympathy. "I think so. Try not to worry, she's in the best place now and I'm sure you'll be the first to know when there's any news."

Huh, it was easy for him to tell us not to worry; his BFF hadn't just been carted off in an ambulance. But I didn't say that. Instead, I let out a long, involuntary sigh.

"You two are probably a bit shaken," Nick said. "Come on, let's go and get a drink in the canteen. Who wants a hot chocolate? I hear that's good for shock."

CHAPTER THIRTEEN

They say good news travels fast – well, bad news travels faster. Scientists should investigate because I am telling you, it is definitely a thing. No sooner had I got home from drama school when my phone beeped and I saw I had a message from Shenice.

Leg broken 🙁 *S xx*

Thirty seconds later, it beeped again. This time it was Molly.

I sat on my bed, staring at my phone. Somewhere in the background, I could hear the faint ring of the house phone but I ignored that. Poor Shenice. She'd worked so hard, first of all to get the role of Tallulah and then to learn all her lines and stage directions, and now she wasn't going to get to play her. And just to put the cherry on top of the sucky cake, she wasn't going to get to kiss Harry's forehead. It wasn't fair. In fact, it sucked big time.

"Cassie?" Mum's voice floated up the stairs. "There's someone on the phone for you."

It would be Molly, I guessed, although she normally called my mobile. Sighing, I went downstairs and took the handset Mum was holding out. "Hello?"

"Cassidy, this is Miss Skelly."

I nearly dropped the phone. What could she want?

And then I realized she must be calling to tell me the show was off.

"Hi, Miss Skelly," I said. "It's very kind of you to phone. Are you calling everyone?"

There was a small silence. "No, just you, darling."

I frowned. Maybe Nick was doing the others. "Oh."

"First of all, I want you to know how very sorry I am to hear about Shenice's leg," Miss Skelly said. "We've never had anything like this happen before. The boys in question have been severely reprimanded. It's terrible for everyone but most importantly for Shenice. I know she's worked very hard."

I thought of the hours we'd spent rehearsing. "Yeah. We all have," I said sadly.

"Which brings me on to my next point," Miss Skelly said, her tone clipped and brisk. Here it comes, I thought, the death blow.

"I've spoken to Shenice and she tells me you've been helping her to learn her lines. In fact, she says you know the part almost as well as she does. Is that correct?"

I stared at the floor in confusion. The conversation had taken a sudden weird turn.

"I suppose so," I answered.

Miss Skelly cleared her throat. "No need to be modest, darling. I seem to remember you did quite a good audition, although your singing needs a bit of work. But there's no time to worry about that now."

I blinked hard. Had she really just said I'd done a good audition? My chest started to puff up with pride. And then her comment about my singing filtered through and everything drooped back down again.

"So?" she went on. "What do you think? Can you do it?"

"Do what?" I asked, now thoroughly bewildered.

"Take over the role," Miss Skelly said in an exasperated voice. "Play Tallulah in the end-of-course production. Because the show must go on, you know. Although I admit it will be difficult to do that if you say no."

This time I really did drop the phone.

"What?" I said slowly, once I'd got it the right way up again. "Let me get this straight — you want me to play Tallulah?"

"That's right," Miss Skelly said. "Shenice is a bit taller than you, of course, but I'm sure wardrobe can fix the dress so no one notices.  You'll have to work hard and there's not much time. But I'm sure everyone will be very grateful if you accept."

Everyone except Shenice, I thought, with a surge of guilt. She wasn't going to be pleased that I was taking her role or that I'd be kissing the leading man instead of her. And she was already jealous of Molly for no reason — how would she feel about me and Harry?

But if I didn't play Tallulah, I'd be letting Molly and everyone else down.

Mum had come to stand next to me, listening as I talked. "Hang on, Miss Skelly." Covering the handset, I stared at Mum. "I don't know what to do."

She gazed at me for a long moment. "Do you think you can do it?"

I shrugged. Running through lines was a lot different to performing them in front of a live audience. "I don't know."

"What's worrying you? Don't you know the part?"

Mentally, I ran through Tallulah's scenes. "Mostly. But I'm scared."

Mum smiled. "If that's all that's holding you back then you should do it. Don't let a little bit of fear stop you – Rolo was scared of the water but that didn't stop him from becoming Rolo the Radical Surfdog, did it?"

Against the odds, I grinned, remembering the first time he'd leaped on top of Alex's board. "No."

"And anyway," Mum said, "your dad will be the first to tell you that a bit of fear is a good thing in a performer. It gives you an edge, keeps you sharp."

Gnawing on a fingernail, I weighed things up. On the one hand, the thought of going onstage as Tallulah filled me with more terror than I'd ever felt in my life. But on the other, I could feel the weight of all the people who'd be disappointed if the performance was cancelled, including one of my very best friends.

Uncovering the phone, I took a deep breath. "Okay, Miss Skelly, I'll do it. I'll be your Tallulah."

Mum pressed a hand on my shoulder and squeezed hard. "Good girl. I'm proud of you."

"Excellent news, Cassidy," Miss Skelly said. "Thank you, darling. As my agent would say, you're a real trooper."

It was only when I'd put the phone down that the enormity of what I'd agreed to do hit home. OMG, I had two days to learn a principal role. Forty-eight hours. 2,880 minutes. Turning on my heel, I took the stairs two at a time and grabbed my mobile to call Molly.

"We've got a major emergency," I told her. "How soon can you get here?"

I don't know if it's possible for someone's head to be so filled with stuff that it actually explodes but mine definitely feels like it could. Since Miss Skelly's phone call yesterday, I have lost count of how many times I've gone over Tallulah's lines. I even woke up saying them. I've also learned that brushing your teeth and speaking are two tasks that are best kept separate – I think I got all the toothpaste out of my hair but that stuff is surprisingly sticky.

I've also stood on the wrong bit of the stage approximately one million times, danced when I am not supposed to dance, not danced when I am supposed to dance, missed my cue so often that I am sure Nick is despairing and failed to kiss Harry five times. Honestly, all I have to do is kiss him on the forehead but it feels like I am stabbing Shenice in the heart every time and I can't do it. I've tried pretending he is Joshua or Ethel and that just made things worse, especially when I accidentally blew a raspberry instead.

It doesn't help that Shenice is ignoring my messages. Molly says that she just needs a bit of time to mourn and come to terms with what's happened but I really don't want her to hate me. So I am doing the best I can and trying to forget how much depends on me NOT MESSING UP.

The only good thing to happen is that Nathan has insisted I need a SUGAR RUSH MOUNTAIN to calm my nerves. We're heading to Shake Shack after school today, although he has agreed to read through the script with me while we eat. Actually, I am not sure I will be able to eat. I can't wait until this is all over.

Nathan's mum gave us a lift into Windsor. She asked me about our holiday and I did my best to answer but my brain was bubbling over from everything and I might have told her I was in the paper instead of Rolo. Once we were in Shake Shack, I pulled out my copy of the script and started to open it. Nathan put his hand on top of the cover. "Ice cream first, work afterwards."

Reluctantly, I nodded. We ordered a Sugar Rush Mountain to share and Nathan sat back in the seat opposite me. "So, tell me about Cornwall. Is the surf as good as everyone says it is?"

I thought back to the golden sands of the beach, the

waves crashing in and washing away again. I remembered the first time I'd popped up on my board, riding a wave to the shore, and how awesome it had felt. And some of my anxiety dropped away. I smiled. "Yeah, it's pretty amazing. How were the waves in Australia?"

"Big," he said. "Too big for me but I watched some really rad surfers take them on. They looked so cool."

Remembering how impressive Alex had looked riding the peak of a wave, I nodded. "I definitely want to go back. Dad says he's been booked to perform there again next year so I think it's looking good."

We swapped holiday stories until the Sugar Rush Mountain arrived, and then there was no time to talk. In amongst the Oreos, the chocolate sauce and the Maltesers was the softest, creamiest vanilla ice cream ever. It was a work of genius and we both felt it deserved our full attention. When it was almost all gone, Nathan sat back and licked his lips. "They don't make sundaes like that in Australia."

"Not in Cornwall, either." I glanced up at him and then looked away before he saw. "There are some things only Windsor can offer."

He smiled. "You can say that again."

My eyes came to rest on the BUGSY MALONE script on top of my bag and I sighed. "I should really look at my lines. Sorry."

"No problem," he said. "Although I should warn you, I'm not great at acting."

I pulled a face. "I'm not sure I am either."

But I opened up the book and shuffled up the seat so

he could sit next to me. We worked through my lines, with Nathan playing everyone except Tallulah so that I got a feel for what was happening.

And then we got to the scene with Bugsy where I had to ask him to smear my lipstick and my heart started to thud.

"I can't do this bit," I mumbled, putting my head in my hands. "Every time I try, I think of Shenice."

Nathan stared at me. "There's a kissing scene?"

I nodded. "Yeah. It's not proper kissing or anything, only a peck on the forehead, but it feels all kinds of wrong, especially when Shenice likes Harry so mu—" I clapped my hand over my mouth. "I'm not supposed to tell anyone about that!"

"You didn't need to," he said. "I've seen how she looks at him."

I didn't have time to worry about that now — I had bigger things to stress about. "I think Nick will explode if I don't get it right tomorrow and I don't want to know what Miss Skelly does to people who disappoint her."

He was silent for a minute. "Can't they just cut it?"

"Not really," I said. "It's kind of important to the plot. Blousey breaks up with Bugsy over it."

Nathan cleared his throat. "But you don't want to do it. Shenice doesn't want you to do it. Harry probably doesn't want to do it, either, if he likes Shenice, and — and..." He looked away and I realized he was the closest I'd even seen him to losing his cool. "Some other people might not like it much either."

I felt my jaw drop. He'd been fine until I'd mentioned the kiss. Surely he couldn't be...JEALOUS?

"But the story doesn't work if Tallulah doesn't kiss Bugsy," I explained. "Blousey has to see it and get angry with him. So — uh — I have to do it somehow. I'm just not sure how at the moment."

He glanced away. "If you have to do it, you have to do it, I guess. It was only an idea."

As the silence got more and more awkward, I shut the script. "I should probably get going."

Without looking at me, Nathan nodded. "Okay. Let me just pay."

I pulled out my purse, not sure if I'd done something wrong, but he waved it away. "No, I'll get this one."

"Only if you let me pay next time," I said, smiling,

but he didn't smile back and a cold feeling squirmed in my tummy that had nothing to do with ice cream.

Judging from the look on Nathan's face, I wasn't sure there would be a next time.

Dear Miss Bond,

Thank you for your letter enquiring about a place at the Queen's Academy of the Dramatic Arts. I am delighted to hear that your drama school production of *Bugsy Malone* is going so well, although obviously saddened to hear that your own success is due to your friend's bad luck. I do agree that in this the case, the phrase "break a leg" seems to have been a portent of doom and wish Shenice well in her recovery.

At present, you are a little young to join us, in spite of being "very nearly twelve", and I suggest that you continue to hone your acting skills for a few more years before contacting us again. Unfortunately, we are unable to accept applications on behalf of animals and if Rolo really is a comedy genius, you might consider seeking

out a professional animal trainer to bring out
this skill. Goodness knows the world needs
more funny dogs.

Nerves are a natural part of performing and
your concern about "freezing harder
than the North Mountain" is understandable.
My advice would be to embrace the adrenaline
rush but try to have fun too.

I wish you the very best of luck with your
performance on the night.

Yours sincerely,
Jane Webb
Admissions Secretary
QADA

Comedy genius

CHAPTER FOURTEEN

Molly messaged me later that evening.

*Shen is home from hospital. Wanna go and
see her? Mxx*

To be honest, I wasn't sure I did. Ordinarily I'd have
been over there like a shot but this is not an ordinary
situation. What if Shenice is upset because she thinks I've
broken the BFF CODE by playing Tallulah? Between
Nathan, my nerves and Shenice, I am starting to think I

should have said no to Miss Skelly.

"Go and see her," Mum told me, when I asked her what to do. "Just be sensitive. She's bound to be disappointed. Imagine how you'd feel if you had got the part you wanted, only to have it snatched away."

When she put it like that I could see her point. If I was in Shenice's shoes, I'd have felt like crying for the rest of my life. Rummaging in the snack cupboard, I found a big bar of Dairy Milk. We were going to need chocolate to get through this.

Shen looked less than happy to see me when we arrived. She hardly even spoke to me for the first ten minutes. I felt like crying.

"Okay," Molly said, once the conversation dried up for the third time. "The atmosphere in here is terrible.

Shen, I know you're upset but there's no need to take it out on Cassie. She's just trying to help."

Shenice pressed her lips together. "I know."

"This is hard for me too, Shenice," I burst out. "I never wanted to take Tallulah away from you."

Shen looked away. "But you did, no matter how it happened."

I took a deep breath. "Is it because I have to kiss Harry? Honestly, Shen, it's not like I want to."

Suddenly, Shenice looked tired. She closed her eyes and I knew she was trying not to cry. "I think you ought to go now."

I looked at her in despair. I started to say something, but Molly shook her head.

"Okay. Maybe we'll see you after the show," she said gently.

Shenice didn't answer. An alarm bell rang in the back of my head. "You are coming to see it, aren't you?"

The silence stretched and stretched.

"I don't know," Shenice said in a small voice. "I don't think I can bear to."

Molly and I didn't say much on the way home – we were both too upset. For Shenice not to come and see us was unthinkable. But there wasn't anything we could do to make her. We'd just have to hope she understood that none of this was my fault.

I had a dream last night that Joshua and Ethel had got hold of my feather boa

229

and were crawling around the living room in it, pretending to be chickens. I woke up in a cold sweat, thinking it was real, before I remembered my costume was hanging in the dressing room and drifted back to sleep. Then I dreamed that Nick was shouting at me because I wouldn't kiss Harry and I pretended he was Rolo to get through it. When I opened my eyes, Rolo had his paws on my pillow and his nose in my eyeball. Honestly, I will be glad when tonight is over.

Rehearsals went a bit better than the day before. The set was finished and it looked amazing — I could almost believe I was in Fat Sam's. This time, I only stood in the wrong place a few times and hardly missed a single cue. There was this one big empty silence and Molly stared at me so hard I thought her eyes would pop out, before I realized it was me and gabbled out my line.

But I still couldn't bring myself to kiss Harry, especially when I knew how unhappy it was making

Shenice and Nathan, not even in costume for the dress rehearsal. Nick's shoulders slumped in defeat. "Can you blow him a kiss, Cassidy? Would that be easier?"

Miserably, I nodded. Everyone was depending on me and yet all I could do when I looked at Harry was freeze, especially now I could feel Nathan's eyes boring into me from the wings.

"I don't bite," Harry said, once we were both offstage.

"No, but Shenice might," I muttered.

We had a two-hour break before we were due back at the theatre for the performance. I went to Molly's for tea and afterwards we warmed up our voices with a round of Singstar. Molly won – she always does – but I like to think I've got a bit better, even if Miss Skelly does think my singing needs work.

By the time we got back into the dressing room, my nerves were strung tighter than Liam's guitar. As I got closer to my chair, I saw a box wrapped with a green ribbon.

"Ooh, you've got a good-luck present!" Molly exclaimed. "Who's it from?"

"My parents, probably," I said, tugging the ribbon off.

Inside the box was the cutest little grey kitten cuddly toy. It had green eyes and a little bell around its neck — $\longrightarrow$ I loved it. There was no label or any kind of message attached but I decided it must have come from Mum and Dad.

"Aw!" Molly said. "Your parents are so sweet. Mine didn't get me anything."

I supposed Molly's family was used to her performing so maybe it wasn't such a big deal to them.

"Her name is Tallulah," I decided, setting the kitten in front of my mirror and hoping she'd bring me luck.

There was a knock at the dressing-room door.

"Into the green room, everyone," the musical director called. "Time for vocal warm-ups."

We hurried out to join everyone and my stomach started to squirm. Vocal warm-ups meant it was half an hour until curtain up. I tried not to worry about what was going to happen next and concentrated on the tongue-twisters and scales we had to sing. Once we were finished, Nick stepped forwards.

"I'm not going to say too much but I wanted to wish you the very best of luck for the performance. Take deep breaths, give it everything but don't forget to have fun."

He fired a reassuring smile around the room and then Miss Skelly took centre stage.

"The smell of the greasepaint...the roar of the crowd...there's nothing quite like it," she began, strolling up and down with her cane clattering the floor as she moved. "Every time you step out in front of an audience, you learn something new about yourself as a performer. Each performance is a journey and, as in life, some are easier than others. But for every single one of you, tonight is a test of your talent and determination. I don't wish to worry you but my agent is in the audience and he is looking for the stars of tomorrow. So smile, never look down and, most importantly, PEE OH OH."

It was almost too much for Molly and me – I actually

had to bite my finger to stop myself snorting out loud. But Miss Skelly wasn't finished. "Now, pick up your **PEE EM AIEES** and get out there and shine." She flourished her hand and her eyes glittered in triumph. "It's show time!"

The room erupted into clapping and whooping. I glanced sideways at Molly and saw she was trying not to giggle. Someone should offer Miss Skelly her own reality TV show — she'd be amazing.

The speaker over the door crackled. "Act One beginners onstage."

"That's me," Molly said and stood up. I gave her a quick hug and wished her luck before she vanished through the door leading backstage.

Miss Skelly appeared in the door frame. "Cassidy, do you have a moment?"

Oh no – what now? Was she going to tell me off for not kissing Harry? "Um...yes?"

She sat beside me and leaned closer. "You seem to have some problems with Harry."

"Yes, I—" I began to explain but she cut me off.

"We don't have time for explanations," she said. "I had hoped this would not be necessary but I am going to share with you a trick I have used many times in my career. It is a closely guarded show-business secret. Can I trust you to tell no one?"

My heart started to thud. "Yes, Miss Skelly."

"Good," she whispered. "There have been times in my youth when I was required to kiss someone I did not wish to kiss, for reasons we will not go into. As you must know by now, the stage relies on trickery to cast its spell –

236

everything about acting is an illusion, magic that the audience believes. But you are not Tallulah, Harry is not Bugsy and no one really gets shot. And so, in an emergency, we can use an illusion to make it seem as though a kiss has happened."

"But Nick said—" I tried again.

"Never mind what Nick has said," Miss Skelly snapped. "Blowing Bugsy a kiss is not sufficient. You must kiss him. Now, darling, listen very carefully. I am going to tell you what to do..."

I sat in silence for a few minutes after Miss Skelly had gone. Sucking in a long slow breath, I counted to ten before letting it out. Miss Skelly was right, Tallulah did have to kiss Bugsy. Sitting out there in the audience were my parents, my brother and 200 other people, who'd paid to see a performance and be transported

back to 1920s New York. Miss Skelly's trick **HAD**
to work.

My phone beeped. I picked it up, expecting a
message from my mum, but Shenice's name flashed
up. With shaking fingers, I opened it.

Good luck, Cassie! I'd say break a leg but I
wouldn't wish that on anyone. Can't wait to
see your Tallulah. S xx

I grinned. Shenice was here – she'd
come! And thanks to Miss Skelly, I had
the perfect way to put her jealousy
over Harry to rest. Picking up a ruby-
red lipstick, I plastered on a thick
layer and made my way to the wings.

The speaker crackled again as the music
started to play. I listened as Harry spoke his first few

lines and then we were off. The opening scene flew by —
the audience laughed as one of Fat Sam's gang got splurged
by Dandy Dan's hoodlums. Then suddenly, I didn't want to
be backstage. I wanted to be in the wings, soaking up the
atmosphere, hearing the audience laugh for real.

The stage lights were hot; I could feel them from
where I stood tucked away behind a curtain at the side of
the stage. The song "Bugsy Malone" played and then Harry
was onstage, telling the audience his story. I wasn't on my
own now; the rest of the cast had joined me, ready to
perform the big show-stopping number — "Fat Sam's Grand
Slam". The lights went down, the stagehands changed the
set and we all hurried into our places around the tables and
chairs of the glammed-up speakeasy. Peering into the
audience, I searched for my family. As the music started,
the lights went up and I plastered a sultry smile on my lips.
For the next hour, I wasn't Cassidy Bond — I was Tallulah
and nothing and nobody would get in my way.

The dance went pretty well, although I'm sure Miss Skelly noticed when the flapper girls ended up facing the back of the stage instead of the front.

Once the song was over, we cleared the stage and let Fat Sam harass his hoodlums. Then Molly began wisecracking with Harry, both of them perfectly in character as Blousey and Bugsy, becoming someone else before my very eyes. It was amazing — never mind the audience buying into the magic, I was starting to fall under its spell too.

The next few scenes zipped by and everything seemed to speed up until it was time — the moment I'd been dreading — the kissing scene. Summoning up Miss Skelly's advice, I put on my best scarlet-lipped Tallulah smile and strutted onstage to Harry.

Even as I delivered my lines I was worrying about what was coming next. Then, out of the corner of my eye,

I saw Molly walk on from stage left and I knew I'd run out of time. For a second, I hesitated, frozen under the lights and then something Alex had said flashed into my mind, about how no one knew what they were doing and everyone was just faking it. Wasn't that exactly what Miss Skelly had meant? Everything about performing was fake. The trick was convincing everyone else it was real.

Leaning towards Harry, I placed my hands either side of his head and pulled him towards me. But instead of planting my lips on his forehead, I slid my thumb across at the last second and kissed that instead. A second later, Molly stamped into Harry's line of vision and he pulled away, his face shocked.

"Blousey!" he cried, jumping up to chase after Molly.

I'd done it! Okay, I hadn't actually kissed Harry but it had looked authentic and the audience had no idea we'd fooled them. The thumb trick Miss Skelly had told me about had worked!

I sashayed offstage, leaving Molly to sing the first of Blousey's solos, a love song called "I'm Feeling Fine". I listened from the wings, amazed all over again at how fantastic she was, even though Fat Sam cut her off early. Surely Miss Skelly's agent would be impressed? I know I'm her BFF, but anyone could see Molly was a star waiting to go supernova.

During the interval we all compared notes. Molly was desperate to know how I'd managed the kiss with Harry but I was under strict instructions from Miss Skelly and my lips were sealed. All I had to do now was get through Tallulah's big number – I'd been so worried about the kiss that I hadn't really had time to think about how it would feel to sing solo. But now that I had to do it, I was

suddenly anxious. I was opening Act Two — what if
I messed this up instead of the kiss?

I stood rooted to the floor beneath my spotlight as
the opening bars played and realized with horror that my
mind had gone blank. What was my opening line? When was
my cue to start singing? Had the band played two bars of
music or four? My stomach churned so hard that I thought
I was going to be sick. I couldn't do this. Somewhere out
there in the audience was the girl who would have wowed
everyone. I was a poor second place.

Desperately, I looked for Shenice, hoping she'd forgive
me for ruining her part. I found her by the door. But she
didn't look worried. Instead, she had the biggest smile on
her face. She lifted one hand and gave me a thumbs up.
She believed in me! She thought I could do it. I'd sing the
song for her, I decided.

There was a fractional pause in the music. I glanced

down at the musical director and he smiled too. And without stopping to think about it any more, I opened my mouth and started to sing.

I wobbled my way through the first line, and then through the second, keeping my eyes on Shenice the whole time. And then a miracle happened – Tallulah started to take over! By the time I'd finished, I was belting it out as though I really was a sassy chanteuse and shimmying around the stage like Fat Sam's girl. When I'd finished, the audience cheered and I'm pretty sure I could hear Shen over everyone else.

I hurried into the wings and bumped into Molly. She pulled me into a fierce hug. "Well done!"

I grinned in the darkness. "Thanks. Your turn now."

By the time Molly had brought the house down with her second heartbreaking solo, the end of the show was in sight. I managed to avoid the worst of the foam in the big splurge-gun finale, but I could see out of the corner of my eye that Harry hadn't been so lucky. The audience loved it though — as we did the final bows, I could see Mum and Dad on their feet, clapping and cheering. I spotted Shenice as well, propped up with her leg in plaster and she had the biggest smile on her face — PHEW! Once the curtain fell, I turned to Molly and hugged her. "We did it! We did it!"

"You were ACES," she said, beaming at me.

"No, you were ACES!" I squealed. "Really really ACES!"

Harry patted me on the shoulder. "Well done, Cassie. That was some smooch."

Molly grinned. "It was. Now spill the beans — how did you do it?"

I summoned up a mysterious smile and gave her the thumbs up. "An old show-business trick Miss Skelly taught me. Sadly, I am sworn to secrecy."

Her eyes widened. "Really?"

I leaned closer. "Okay. Maybe I'll tell you later."

Molly grinned. "Got ya. Come on, let's get out of these costumes." She adopted a dramatic pose. "As Miss Skelly would say, our public awaits!"

CHAPTER FIFTEEN

I think I might have floated from the dressing room
to the bar after the show, although it could have been
the fumes from the industrial-strength make-up wipes
that made me light-headed, rather than the buzz of
performing. When I looked at Molly, she had this kind
of glow about her, as though someone had lit a lantern
inside her. Harry had it too, and one or two of the others.
I didn't feel like I was glowing. I was just glad I'd made
it through without any major mistakes.

The person I most wanted to see was Shenice. She was sitting with a glass of Coke, her broken leg sticking out in front of her and two crutches by her side.

"Don't get up," I said, bending down to hug her.

"You were great," she said, hugging me back. "Awesome work."

"Pah," I said, shrugging. "I got through it. You'd have been better."

She glanced at me sideways. "Oh, I don't know. That kiss with Harry was pretty convincing."

I shook my head. "It was all a trick. We didn't really kiss."

"Cass, it's okay," she said in a soothing tone. "Whatever you did, it rocked."

I studied her suspiciously. "I'm so glad you came. What changed your mind?"

She smiled. "I had a visit from Harry and...I might have asked him about you. And, no offence, but he told me there was only one Tallulah he wanted to kiss!"

My eyes widened as though it was the worst insult ever but inside I was laughing. "Huh, that's rude."

"Isn't it? But I wouldn't have missed my best friends' big moment anyway." She held out a permanent marker. "Now, any chance of an autograph or are you too famous?"

"Anything for a fan, darling," I drawled, and scribbled my name on her plaster cast.

Molly rushed over, looking like all of her birthdays and Christmases had come at once. "I don't believe it. I don't BELIEVE IT!"

There's only one thing that could possibly get Molly this excited, apart from a declaration of love from Liam, and that's something to do with singing. Shenice and I looked at each other. "You got scouted!" we burst out at exactly the same moment.

"YES!" Molly shrieked. "Miss Skelly's agent wants to talk about about signing me up! He thinks I've got a bright future in musical theatre."

"No way!" Shenice breathed.

"Yes way!" I yelled, high-fiving both of them.

My family hurried over to congratulate us. "Well done," Mum said, planting a big squashy kiss on my cheek before I could stop her. "We're so proud of you."

"Another musical prodigy," Dad said, giving me a quick squeeze. "If Joshua and Ethel are any good we could be Windsor's answer to the Von Trapp family."

Liam rolled his eyes. "I suppose you didn't totally suck." He glanced over at Molly, who was talking to her parents and Miss Skelly. "Molly was pretty good, though."

WOW — coming from Liam that was practically a compliment. And a double win for Molly, because he'd remembered her name AND noticed how amazing she'd been. I filed it away to tell her later. "Thanks for the cuddly toy, Mum."

She frowned. "What cuddly toy?"

I rolled my eyes. "The one you left in the dressing room. So cute."

Mum shook her head. "Sorry, Cassie, it wasn't me. Sounds like you've got a mystery admirer."

And then Nathan was standing next to me, shifting from one foot to the other.

"It was from me. I hope you liked it," he said, looking about as shy and uncomfortable as I'd ever seen him. "It was my way of saying sorry for being a green-eyed monster."

Suddenly everything made sense. "I loved it," I said, smiling. "Thank you."

His face lit up. "Good. And well done. For everything. You really pulled it off."

"It wasn't bad, was it?"

He nodded. "It was great. You were great." His eyes shone. "Amazing, actually."

"Thanks," I said, beaming back at him.

And right at that moment, I didn't think anything could be better. Shen hadn't played her dream role but she'd still got the boy, although I'm sure she could have done without the broken leg. It looked like Molly was on her way to superstardom and me – well, I might have faked it and fooled the audience into buying the illusion, but I'd faced my fear and survived. And I hadn't even thrown up once. I'm not sure acting is really my thing, and singing definitely isn't, but one way or another I had a lot of fun sharing the limelight with my besties. In fact, this summer hasn't been the total disaster I thought it would be. Predicting the future isn't my big talent either.

But you know what? Being a BFF just might be!

The End

MEET
TAMSYN MURRAY

* Tamsyn's special talent is writing and she is the author of many books for young readers.
* Tamsyn was born in Cornwall and loves going back to visit whenever she can.
* Tamsyn's most embarrassing onstage moment was falling off a swing in front of all her school friends, aged seventeen.
* Tamsyn's not-so-secret wish is to perform in London's West End.
* Tamsyn's weirdest talent is being able to lick her own elbow.

www.tamsynmurray.co.uk

TAMSYN'S
SPECIAL AWARDS

* BEST HUSBAND: Lee Slater
* BEST CHILDREN: T & E
* BEST AGENT: Jo Williamson
* BEST EDITOR: Stephanie King
* BEST SUPPORTING EDITOR: Sarah Stewart
* BEST PR: Amy Dobson and Hannah Reardon
* BEST ILLUSTRATOR: Antonia Miller
* BEST DESIGNER: Sarah Cronin
* BEST SET DESIGN: Hendra Holiday Park, Newquay
* BEST SOUNDTRACK: Bugsy Malone (various artists)
* BEST SUPPORTING GROUP: Loughton Operatic Society

CATCH UP WITH
COMPLETELY CASSIDY

Check out the latest gossip at
www.completelycassidy.co.uk